Ascendant: Online
Book 1
Witness the Beginning

By: Joseph DeProfio
©2020

Contents

Prologue: The Gambit

"He can't be serious!" Auren heaved the missive across his chamber as he shot out of bed. Ignacious was letting the title "King of the Gods" get to his head. The King's decision to put humanity to the sword could not come to pass.

Auren's feet slapped against the marble floors of the Grand Hall as he raced to the King's chambers. He had not taken the time to "dress" for the occasion, opting for his crimson toga and a simple circlet. Appearing before the king, Ignacious, had become a matter of ceremony. Within the last century, nothing short of regalia had been deemed appropriate by the King's inner circle. Auren's firm belief that billions of mortal souls were worth more than dressing to impress allowed him to press on undaunted.

The great brass doors parted easily, and to Auren's surprise, the King's chamber was packed. Gods of all stations had arrived to voice their discontent at his decision to eradicate the human race. Auren's arrival seemed to be the dramatic pause in the conversation that Ignacious was waiting for, as he stood from his lounging position on the throne.

"Now, now. I'm sure that you are all here to call for the crown to be taken from me. Humanity is everyone's favorite project, after all, hear me out for a moment, and all will be explained."

Auren seethed.

It was no surprise that Ignacious would try to smooth over his decision with the rest of the gods that had gathered; smooth-talking had gotten him this far.

"Humanity has doomed itself, a perpetual war based on silly differences that don't matter in the much grander scheme of things have set them far behind the other sentient species in their universe, many of which are capable of Interstellar travel while the humans have yet to colonize their own Moon. What I am proposing will grant the Humans a quick and painless death instead of a war they're not equipped to participate in. I say this would be a kindness, what say you?"

An eerie hush fell over the crowd of gods. "What about the Ascendant Program?" Auren shouted, his frustration finally getting the better of him.

"Most of the humans have rejected any sort of 'faith', which the Ascendant Program requires to function," Ignacious said with a dismissive wave of his hand and not so much as a look in Auren's direction.

"That's bullshit and you know it!" The crowd around Auren parted. Standing so close to one who would defy the King was political suicide.

An oppressive wave of essence poured out of the god, activating as his rage piqued. Auren's Battle Aura, his namesake, was active.

The Battle Aura amplified the brash god's prowess in combat and increased his pain tolerance significantly. When the Battle Aura was active Auren became an engine of destruction.

Ignacious didn't flinch. Behind the veneer of calm and confidence, Auren saw the wavering of his resolve.

"That's enough, Auren, stand down." A cold, sturdy hand pressed into his shoulder. Morkhan, the venerable vizier, had spoken. "This is for the best." *Come outside,* Morkhan's voice spoke into Auren's mind. The Battle Aura flared for a moment before quenching. The firm-handed vizier led Auren out of the chamber. The dull roar of gossip muffled as Morkhan sealed the brass doors behind the pair.

"You've grown reckless in your station, Auren, you must-"

"Temper my power with even judgment. I remember," Auren finished. Morkhan had taught him much. Mastery of his passion was not something another could teach him, no matter how venerable.

"You may be on to something though, with the Ascendant Program." Auren arched his eyebrows in surprise. "Sure, the levels of faith required to preserve the entirety of the human race are not present, but we could preserve, say, a thousand through the program? Maybe enough to empower, manage, and then lead against a delusional and tyrannical god?"

"What?" tumbled out of Auren's slackened jaw.

"We will need to act with purpose. Ignacious's plan will take some time to come to fruition with the hurdles I have put in his way. Now pick your jaw up off the floor and help an old god put one of his students back in check, will you?"

Chapter I: Get in the Game

The doorbell's tone punctuated Tony's listless slumber.

What time is it? he wondered. Tony stripped the blanket off the bed as he sat up. He cleared the sleep from his eyes and grabbed a hoodie, then wandered in the direction of the door of his one-bedroom apartment, searching for pants.

His abode was sparsely decorated. Some of the posters he had managed to salvage from his room at his parents' house were hung on the walls of his bedroom, the "kitchen" was made up of a digital griddle, e-class Ingrediprep unit, and a sink all on the same countertop. The living area was even more shameful to look at, but Tony managed to locate his favorite pair of sweatpants on the third-hand sofa that leaned against the wall.

Adjacent to the slumped couch was one of Tony's prized possessions, the Gambit Games Multi-Console projector. The scattered trophies from years of youth sports and martial arts tournaments rested on a dusty shelf to "round out" the feel of the space. The digital chime continued to sound. Whoever was at the door wouldn't be leaving until he answered, he noted, hopping toward the door, one leg in his sweats, the other struggling to find purchase. "Be right there!"

Tony pulled on his pants, unbolted the door, and flung it open. "What?" he shouted into the face of the mailroom worker of the complex. She was tall, athletically built with sandy-colored cascades of hair, flawless sandstone skin, and eyes so blue he could swim in them. He always intended to ask her name and see if she wanted to get a coffee with him sometime.

Most of their interactions had been limited to Tony dropping off rent checks and signing for packages, he couldn't help but feel like there was potential chemistry between them.

Probably explosive chemistry, like the volatile kind, you dunce. Now stop staring and say something!

"S-sorry, I was err- asleep," he admitted.

Real smooth, Romeo.

Her eyebrow arched beyond the slim ebon frame of her glasses and Tony felt a sweat break out across his back. "It's noon. You have a package to sign for. Looks fancy."

Noon? Tony took the tablet in hand and initialed with his index finger without a thought before the mail attendant thrust the package into his hands and left.

It was heavy.

"Thank you," he called after her.

For a moment, Tony considered jogging after her. Everyone else in the Multiplex was out for the day or already buckled down to work, so if he made an ass out of himself it would only be the two of them. He decided against it and nudged the door switch with his foot. The door swung closed and hissed as the hydraulics built into the springs kept it from closing.

Someday, he thought. *Maybe when I drop off this month's rent?*

Tony placed the package on his dining room table, the bridge between the kitchen and the living space. A flimsy thing made out of pine that was better suited to holding outstanding bills and junk mail than sitting for a meal. He never really had anybody over anyway and it was just as easy to plop down on the dilapidated sofa and eat while streaming *Spider-Man: The Other* for the umpteenth time. His heart froze for half a second as he read the shipping label.

To: Antonious King
District 6, Building A, Sublevel A, Apartment 13
Elko, NV 89801

No one called him Antonious anymore, not since the last argument with his father almost a year ago. He shook the thing. There were no clunks, and its contents were well packed.

From: Gambit Games c/o Ascendant Online
1 GG Place
Hollywood, CA 90028

"What the?" Tony couldn't help but say aloud. Gambit Games had won Indie Developer of the Year Award in 2030 with their RTS "Godmaker," and won the 2037 "Game Studio Triple Threat" award.

After the micro-transaction fiasco in the gaming community that ran late into the 20s, consumers were hesitant to trust a new AAA studio. Gambit Games had taken the industry by storm with immersive stories, fresh mechanics, and exceptional graphics without VR support. Ascendant Online hadn't released yet, set for a summer 2038 release. AO wouldn't be the first VR MMO, but it would be the first put out by Gambit. The release of their "Multi-Console" had revolutionized console gaming, allowing players to relive the classics, all the way back to first-gen XBOX and PS2 games. Beyond that, the tech allowed seamless cross-platform support with the primary consoles put out by Microsoft, Sony, Nintendo, and could even bridge with current-gen PC servers.

With feverish excitement, Tony grabbed hold of the first instrument he found to open the package. The spoon was resting next to last night's empty ice cream carton and carved into the tape securing the box, freeing its contents and a handful of packing peanuts. Resting on top of a matte-black box, emblazoned with Gambit Games' branding, was a letter.

No one sends letters anymore! he thought, the tips of his fingers running over the coarse parchment. The Gambit Games seal had been almost punched into the paper and the signature at the bottom was in ink, *from a pen.*

Hello, Antonious!

Congratulations! You have been selected to participate in the exclusive closed beta of Ascendant Online! Contained you will find the Gambit Games Mark II Pro Headset with Ascendant Online preloaded. You will also find three starter codes to grant initial class gear in-game and your own beta tester title code! This will mark your character as one of the very first and enable you to transfer your beta character to the retail version of Ascendant Online upon release!

Welcome to the Ascendant Program, Antonious, see you in-game!

Auren Brandt
Gambit Games CEO

Tony couldn't believe it. He'd signed up for the closed beta when he pre-ordered AO with no hopes of being accepted. Gambit Games was a giant in the industry, and they were only accepting three hundred players into the beta. He dashed over to the screen built into the wall next to his door, unlocked it, and opened the "My Schedule" app. He breathed a sigh of relief.

Working third shift had its perks. Minimal interaction with people, decent housing benefits, and a killer shift differential; however, it did next to nothing for remembering what day it was, they all bled together. Tony worked Tuesday to Saturday, and it was an afternoon on Monday. He would have time to play right away.

Without missing a beat, he went back to the table and exhumed the headset. It was a thing of beauty, the same matte black as the box it came in. The Gambit Games logo, two interlocking G's with a 6-sided die at the merger of the two letters, inlaid with gold at either side of the visor. Turning it over in his hands, the health advisory and disclaimer paperwork tumbled out into the box. No one ever read that stuff and he had no intention of wasting the time to do so now.

Tony retrieved the power supply and charging cable from the box and rushed into his room, flinging the door open, scattering laundry and rippling the posters haphazardly tacked to the plain cream walls. He plugged the cord into the outlet at the head of his bed and the other end into the receiver at the top of the headset. The optimal setup for a full VR experience. A small red dot illuminated, it was charging and ready to go. Tony lay down on his bed and pulled the headset on. He blinked, and the headset powered on — the nodes lining the inside, detecting a user.

The landing screen itself, only a partial VR environment, took him out of the shoddy apartment in the basement of the Multiplex housing hundreds of thousands of people and onto a coastal Elysian field.

Ascendant Online – Closed Beta

The words hung in front of him, just over the lapping waves on the coast. Tony focused on the flashing "Launch" button, and the headset complied. The familiar tingle of the VR integration crawling over his scalp and a subtle chill running through his body.

"Welcome to Ascendant Online. Please, select your starting class."

Chapter II: Paradox of Choice

Tony's mouth dropped open, agape with disbelief. "Only three classes?" he muttered.

Acolyte: A novice of magical disciplines. Acolytes develop their power through research into the principles of spellcraft.
Advancement beyond level 5 allows for specialization options.
Squire: A novice of martial disciplines. Squires refine their prowess through continued exposure to combat and training.
Advancement beyond level 5 allows for specialization options.
Apprentice: A novice of skilled disciplines. Apprentices further themselves through non-combat encounters and the clever utilization of skills.
Advancement beyond level 5 allows for specialization options.

His mind raced. *Are there only three classes in the beta? Do Specializations unlock more classes? If specs are first at level 5, do you get more every five levels? What is max level?*

"One thing at a time," he reminded himself. Gambit Games had chosen him to help test the beta, not to analyze their design choices.

Playing a rogue archetype character was out of the question; after the re-re-release of *Skyrim Ultimate Edition* Tony had sworn off "sneak-archer" since that was what every character he made for the classic game ended up as.

Mage-type characters were often some of the highest damage dealers a game could produce, but Mages were tough for solo play due to their typically lackluster defense and survivability.

Summoned pets or constructs could usually make up for that, but he didn't want to manage his own resources and keep track of an elemental or imp in combat.

That left him with the "Squire" option, but it just seemed so lame. Did starting as a Squire mean that he was beholden to some crusty old Knight? That he would be stuck carrying flags and doing fetch quests until he could specialize?

Tony pushed those thoughts aside and focused on the Squire option. He was sure that every starting class would have their minutia to deal with in the starting quests, but he wanted to experience everything that Gambit Games had to show him in Ascendant Online, up close and personal.

Squire Class Selected. Please select a Character Customization Option:
Express Customization | Manual Customization
Headset Sync Customization (Recommended)
Use Preset Characters

Headset Sync was the obvious choice. A majority of VRMMO games had a similar feature. The headset would read the facial features of the user, use the front-mounted cameras to get a rough body composition scan and place a near-perfect recreation onto the in-game avatar. Gambit Games did most things better than their competitors. Tony couldn't wait to see how this came out; he focused on Headset Sync Customization.

> You have selected Headset Sync Customization. Would you like to continue?
> **This selection is final.**

That's a weird place for confirmation, Tony thought as he mentally affirmed.

> As the headset scans, users may experience mild discomfort. Please do not remove the headset until the scan is complete.

The hair on the back of Tony's neck stood on end. Every instinct fired a warning; something about this was off. He couldn't place what about the headset saying that he could experience *mild discomfort* made him so uncomfortable.

The sync started and Tony felt the familiar tingle of initial headset boot creep over his scalp and travel down the surface of his skin. When it reached his toes, a wave of bitter cold rebounded back up. Tony's jaw locked, and his eyes slammed shut.

I should have read the disclaimer paperwork!

The cold lingered for what felt like hours before Tony opened his eyes again. His formerly rictus frame instantly relaxed, finding himself in a bed that was hundreds, no, thousands of times more comfortable than his own.

The sheets covering him were the blissful marriage between satin and velvet without the static or clinginess of either.

Hesitant to leave the comfort of the bed, Tony peeked out from under the blankets. The room was covered in tapestries depicting ancient battles and victories of the gods over the Titans and their tyrannical masters, decorated with vases containing flowers and plants the likes of which he had never seen outside of a history book, and furnished with lavish seating and storage. Realization struck.

He was in the game world.

Tony shot out of the bed and rushed to the balcony, just past the elaborate mahogany dresser on the far wall from the bed. Constellations, planets, and stars that he had never seen dotted a gradient violet backdrop. Deep purples, blots of whites, pinks, and even a few streaks of green made up the space right outside his room. He reached out and his fingers brushed against a static field.

Well, at least I won't tumble into space, he thought.

There were three different suns at the center of the Galaxy, one blue, one red, and one white. Tony knew that Gambit Games tried to break the mold with every title they put out, but no one had done Space Opera in a *very* long time.

A notification flashed in the corner of his vision, Tony focused on it, and a shimmering white window appeared before him.

> Soul Sync Completed. Traits have uploaded and await your approval.
> Welcome to the Ascendant Program.

That's a neat touch, Tony thought. "Character Sheet," he said. The notification was replaced with another window.

Name: Antonious King   Title: N/A   Race: Human (Ascendant)

Age: 18   Class: Squire (1)   Specializations: None
Essence: 1(Dormant)

> Would you like to review your pending traits?
> Yes   No

Tony sighed as he focused on the affirmative option. It always took so long to get into the meat of the game from a fresh character. His eyes widened a second later as he read through the rest of his available character sheet.

Attribute Modifiers:

+1 Endurance – Late Shift Worker   -1 Charisma – Clueless Flirt
+1 Strength – Former Athlete   +2 Dexterity – Martial Arts Training
+1 Wits – Quick Thinker   -1 Wisdom – Hot-Headed
+3 Spirit – Survivor

Trait and Background Modifiers

(Progress through the Campaign to Unlock More!)
Familiar – Spirit-Tied Pet (Complete Ascendant Training to Unlock this Trait)
Unseen Ally – [Invalid FeTcH ID: Initiate]
Double-Edged Sword Aptitude – Ancestral Heritage
Ascendant Healing Factor – Ascendant Program Initial Training Required to Unlock
Ascendant Attribute Enhancement – Pending Completion of Ascendant Program Training

Character Sheet:

Attributes

Strength: 11   Charisma: 9   Intelligence: 10

Dexterity: 12   Wisdom: 9   Wits: 11

Endurance: 11   Spirit: 13   Luck: 10

Skills: Complete Ascendant Training to Unlock Skill Ranks

"I have never felt so called out by a video game as I do right now." Indignance and a dash of sarcasm coated every word. "Clueless Flirt? Hot-Headed? I mean, I know that about me, but you don't get to know that about me!" he said, pointing an accusatory finger at his character sheet.

He looked older and of a more powerful build, like the system had put him into prime shape but given him a couple of years in the process. He had always been athletic as a kid, not by choice, but he had slacked on his training during his junior and senior years in high school. He didn't see the point; he was stronger and faster than most of the varsity players on the soccer and football teams and there was only so much training he could do in a high school gym before it turned into self-induced torture.

Tony sighed. "Guess it's time to find the Ascendant Trainer," he said as he dismissed his character sheet with a wave. He went back inside the main part of his room, already twice as large as his apartment, and moved over to the dresser.

He rifled through the drawers and found a variety of clothing, togas, jumpsuits, robes, there was a lot. Tony found some black leather pants, a white linen shirt, and some socks which he put on, grateful that the system had spawned him in bed with underwear.

Once he was dressed, he checked the rest of the drawers and found a sizeable box with "Antonious" scrawled on it. He opened it and found a set of armor inside. To the touch, it was leather, but it felt heavier and tingled in his grasp. Without a second thought, he put on the armor, tunic first, then pants, boots, belt, and wristguards. Before he got the chance to adjust the armor manually it shifted and formed to his body, stretching tight across his musculature but allowing for a full range of motion.

Eyebrow raised, Tony reviewed his equipment screen:

Squire's Training Set
    Helmet: Empty
    Neck: Empty
    Chest: Squire's Training Tunic | +5 Defense Rating
    Shoulders: Empty
    Wrist: Squire's Training Vambraces | +2 Defense Rating
    Rings: Empty
    Hands: Empty
    Waist: Squire's Training Belt | +1 Defense Rating
    Legs: Squire's Training Greaves | +5 Defense Rating
    Feet: Squire's Training Boots | +2 Defense Rating
Set Bonus:

> 2 of 6: Squire's Surety: +10% Damage Reduction
> 4 of 6: Squire's Confidence: +10% Defense Rating
> 6 of 6: Equip the Squire's Training Helm and Gauntlets to Unlock!

The Defense Rating bonuses were meager, at best, but the set bonuses made up for it. While he didn't expect to get armor with set bonuses right from the beginning of the game, Tony wondered why the gloves and helmet weren't included or if they even existed. There were a lot of slots for worn equipment, what two slots finished out the set?

Wrangling his wandering mind, Tony determined that wading in and out of combat wouldn't be entirely life-threatening with the four pieces he had and some decent weapons. It was time to move on and get through whatever tutorial there was so he could get into the meat of the game.

Something caught in the corner of his vision — a mirror. The rendering from the headset was remarkable.

He looked almost *exactly* like himself: jade-green eyes stared back at him, glancing over his olive skin, paled from too much time inside, a mop of black hair rested on top of his head. He pulled back some of the wavy charcoal mess above his left eye, and sure enough, the scar just under his hairline was there. He smirked in the mirror's reflection, satisfied.

Tony started toward the door; a mass of iron that seemed out of place amongst the rest of the lavish decor. There were some intricacies to the metal, but the whole thing looked like it was hewn from one massive slab. The glyphs looked to be roughed in with a hammer while the inscriptions on the walls and floors had been carved with scalpel-like precision.

"You about ready to go? The fate of mankind is a little more important than a fancy mirror," a man said, leaning against the door frame.

Tony hadn't seen or heard anyone come in. The man was tall and muscular, wearing a crimson toga and a burning circlet to keep back unruly, literally flaming hair. His eyes shone like the heart of a roaring bonfire and the vast amounts of his visible skin were deeply tanned. Auren, Lord of Auras, the protagonist of "Godmaker" stood before him.

"There's no time to waste. Let's go."

Chapter III: It Takes Class

Tony stared in awe. He had hundreds of hours logged in "Godmaker" on his Steam account. "Um, yes," was the best he could muster. In "Godmaker" Auren had been a demigod, the rogue-like real-time-strategy experience had endless replay value; a smattering of different endings, different discoverable hero units, hidden side quests, hidden alternate *main quests*, secret artifacts, and resource deposits were just a few reasons why Tony had played the game over and over again. The plot of "Godmaker" had taken Auren and a group of his trusted friends and accumulated allies on their quest to overthrow their titanic overlords and liberate the cosmos from their stranglehold.

Tony's favorite ending in "Godmaker" had not been the viral sensation that showed the vizier Morkhan manipulating the "guile tank" Ignacious into assumed power, but the ending where Auren and the others had ascended to complete godhood and ushered in an era of prosperity and peace, truly taking the game's namesake.

Reminiscing about the game he spent so many hours playing, Tony couldn't help but wonder if the specialization that Ignacious used in "Godmaker" would be available as a Class Specialization later.

The "Chicaner" class was functionally the same as an advanced sword-and-board warrior, but swapped in Charisma Modifiers instead of Stamina, and did not require shields to tank an encounter effectively. The forums had called Ignacious "blusterwall" as a joke referring to some song that released in nineteen ninety-five.

"Let's get a move on," Auren said.

Tony complied, following a pace behind the god. The two of them moved through what Tony soon discovered was the flagship Haght'anak. The metal halls were the same hewn iron as the door of Tony's chamber and the viewports looked into the same gradient space, but with visible "glass" coverings. Questions soared through his mind. There was so much that he wanted to know that Auren might be able to answer.

The halls were busy, people bustling back and forth. Sets of glowing dots could be seen above almost all of them. A majority were white, silver, and blue and very few of them were gold. Tony almost missed the silver color, as it was very difficult to distinguish from the white.

Tony focused on one of the people chatting in the hallway with a white glowing point above them. She was tall and thin, with a sharpness to her curves, pointed ears, stark white hair that fell from her head like a waterfall, and softly glowing silver eyes.

Name: Esava   Level: 3   Race: Celestial Elf (Ascendant)
Class: Acolyte   Essence: 1 (Dormant)

He decided that he would need to figure out what the dots meant. There had been hero units in "Godmaker" that were elves, but they had been some of the more difficult to unlock and even more complicated to fully utilize. He scanned for a blue dot next.

Name: D'jorrin   Level: 2   Race: Burning Ashtar
(Ascendant)
Class: Apprentice   Essence: 1 (Dormant)

Tony had no idea what Ashtar was, but they were tall and broad people, and the "burning" referred to the obvious elemental aspects. D'jorrin's eyes burned out of their sockets like torches and as Tony watched him talk, he noted that the inside of his mouth looked like the heart of a furnace. When the man got excited, his back and shoulders would flare with flames for a moment or two before receding.

It took a couple of turns down different halls for the crowds to thin and Tony to pick out a silver orb instead of a white one, but he managed to.

At first, Tony couldn't entirely tell what he was looking at. The person he looked at was of average human height and shape, but they were androgynous in appearance with short-cropped translucent hair that mirrored the gray-silver of their skin.

As soon as Tony focused on the person to look at their "nameplate" they looked over their shoulder at him, revealing one of their large eyes, a dark-blue orb with flecks of white and silver dotting it like stars.

Name: Jael   Level: 4   Race: Selenian (Ascendant)

Class: Apprentice   Essence: 1 (Dormant)

At Tony's prolonged gaze, Jael turned to face him. When their eyes met Tony found it difficult to look away, like Jael was peering directly into his mind. This was made even more difficult as Jael's body seemed to rearrange itself as Tony watched, forming into a near-exact visage of the admin from his Multiplex.

"What the?" he said. Auren stopped and looked back, then smirked at the confused look on Tony's face.

"Snap out of it, kid, we have places to be!" Auren said with a little too much excitement as he grabbed Tony by the bicep and dragged him away.

"Who… or what was that?" Tony asked.

"That was a Selenian, they're from the Andromeda Galaxy, the one right next door to Earth's. Selenians have an innate talent that they can use to take on the appearance of someone you find attractive."

Tony's face flushed at the explanation.

"Jael there is probably one of the most talented Selenians we've got in the program. All it takes is a moment of eye contact and they can use it. Most Selenians need to at least have a conversation with a person before using the talent effectively," Auren explained.

Tony did a mental double-take. "Wait, so is Jael more than one person, or were you just talking about talented Selenians being able to use the talent with eye contact?"

Auren chuckled softly. "Sorry about that, Selenians don't have a gender until they assume one. I was using they as a singular pronoun."

Tony pressed the edge of his left thumbnail into the tip of his index finger and kicked himself mentally.

"Don't worry about it, Tony, you're fresh out of cryosleep, no one is going to expect you to know the ins and outs of social graces right away," Auren said, giving Tony a light punch on the shoulder.

"Right," Tony responded.

Auren could sense Tony's dour mood and decided to change the subject, trying to lift the boy's spirits. "A lot of Trainers will make a big deal about Ascendant Training. They're exaggerating. The Ascendant Program was *designed* for humans. Most of the trainers we have are either Elves, Ashtar, and if you're lucky, you might get a God or two.

Most of the humans we saved are still in cryo, and the program had to be altered for the others. It should be a breeze for you."

"Hold on, what do you mean 'the humans you saved?' What happened to the rest of the humans?" Tony noted the rising pitch in his voice and took a deep breath.

This is just a game, this is just a game, he reminded himself.

Auren took a deep breath and explained, "In 2038, I started a ploy against Ignacious, the current 'King of the Gods.' He found out about my little scheme earlier than I would have hoped. The carnage he set forth on your planet..." Auren shuddered; a tempest of emotions flashed over his face. Rage, loss, frustration, and melancholy fed into the crackling energy of the Battle Aura trying to ignite over Auren's crossed arms.

"It was terrible," he continued. "You and three hundred others were all I could gather before The Desolation. Since then, members of other sentient races have come to our side, rallied against Ignacious."

"But if the Ascendant Program was designed for humans, why are other races joining the fight? Wouldn't they be safe?" Tony's "plot hole" senses were blaring and the question tumbled out of his mouth before he had the chance to think about it.

"After Earth, we had to alter the Program. We simply wouldn't have the numbers to go against Ignacious and the Cadre of Judgement." Auren's face evened out, setting to a more neutral mood as he discussed the pain points within his plan. "The defining trait of your kind is its versatility, Antonious. We're lucky that it has been to our benefit. The presence of a soul yields sentience in organic creatures, from hounds to humans, this cannot be denied. The modifications allowed for any being with a soul to be compatible with the Program. It is not always a perfect fit, but we do what we must."

"But why are they rallying? What is Ignacious doing?" Tony pressed.

Auren's face darkened, his mouth forming into a thin line before parting to speak again. "Ignacious has dispatched the Cadre of Judgement into the cosmos, eradicating any species that can Ascend that will not join him instead. All. Sentient. Life. Antonious."

— Auren's jaw set. There was no way that Tony could know everything the Lord of Auras had said was true. There was no way for him to know that the "headset sync" option had torn the soul from his body before The Desolation occurred. There was no way for him to know that it had taken fifteen hundred years to rebuild Antonious King in a way that would survive Ascension. The boy wasn't ready for that. —

Tony let out a low whistle. *That's one hell of a way to explain the "closed beta."*

A quest has been added to your Quest Log:
Usurp the Mad King

Chapter IV: Power Leveling

Humanity's last stand rests with the Ascendant Program. As one of the few remaining Humans, you are to gain strength and unite against Ignacious, The Mad King.
Rewards: Title: King Slayer, Experience, Unique Traits

Tony regarded the expanding quest log hovering in the corner of his vision. "Usurp the Mad King." He read the title over again and frowned. The quest had no objective, no requirement that would mark it as complete. Most games would have a defined condition, "Kill X NPC," "Obtain McGuffin and deliver to said person." Nothing like that was in the description of the quest. This frustrated him immensely.

So all I have to do is kill Ignacious?

He did note that the "Completed Quests" tab was pulsing gently as if it were trying to get his attention. Tony focused on it.

The quest log scrolled over to "The Desolation." The quest registered as completed, but it also noted he would have to speak with Auren again to reap the reward of standing around and listening to the game spew exposition. The whole thing gave him the creeps. Space-Opera-Post-Apocalyptica was not what Tony had been expecting from "Ascendant Online" but here he was.

"So, what now?" Tony asked.

"Now," Auren started, "we get you to your Trainer." The god put a reassuring hand on his shoulder and guided him down the hallway. "Then, we'll rush you through the initial quests, and then get you right into the action."

Tony couldn't help but smirk. He had always been into "high risk; high reward" gaming. Most games would advise a cautious approach to the world. Yet, the fact remained that he was encouraged by the AI to play how he preferred.

Part of him couldn't help but wonder if this had been part of the "Headset Sync." Maybe his play data from other Gambit Games titles had been uploaded to his Ascendant Online profile?

Questions for later.

Auren continued down the hall ushering Tony at arm's reach in front of him. Before long, the sounds of combat reached his ears. Spells detonating, the crackling of essence in the air, and the frenzied metronome of steel clashing against steel. At first, Tony thought they were under attack; upon reaching the hangar of the flagship, he discovered that it was repurposed into a massive training facility.

At least twelve different sparring pits stood where starfighters and transports should have been.

Semi-solid holograms sprinted in and out of cover in a handful of live-fire courses, buzzers and announcers blared, and the occasional brass bell could be heard at the end of an obstacle course, the likes of which *Ninja Warrior* could only hope to replicate.

The scene before Tony was complete and utter chaos. His heart thumped against his ribs with his mounting excitement.

Wait a second, I shouldn't be able to feel my heartbeat in here, should I? Tony thought.

"That one," Auren said, cutting off his train of thought as he pointed to a pit toward the middle of the hangar, "your trainer is at Pit Eight. Let's see what you can do."

Tony nodded and jogged off toward the pit; he was used to fighting to prove himself. He pushed his way angrily through the crowd as memories of his father watching coldly from the bleachers during his martial arts tournaments burning in his mind. Cheers of victory meshed with gasps of shock and surprise and roared in his ears. After a lot of shoving, a couple ducked punches, and a whole lot of shouting Tony reached the edge of the pit and looked down at the combatants.

There were two in the pit. One of them was at least a head taller than Tony and his set of Squire's armor was a tattered mess of what it had been. Bruises and small cuts stood out on the large Squire's exposed flesh and a gold dot shone over his head.

Name: Tolik   Level: 6*   Race: Human (Ascendant)

Class: Squire   Specialization: Duelist   Essence: 2

Tolik was the first person that Tony had seen and been able to focus on with a gold point above their head. The fact that there was no (Dormant) descriptor next to the Essence trait in the nameplate that popped up was connected, though Tony wasn't entirely sure how.

Tolik looked like Ivan Drago and Xena had a baby and sent him to Hercules to train. He was absolutely massive and Tony would have been surprised if there were more than ten pounds of fat on the man. The brown hair on top of his head was plastered to the sides of it by sweat, and Tony caught the glint of hazel eyes as he traced his opponent's movements.

The other duelist, an Earth-aspected Ashtar, glided across the ground on a wave of dirt and rocks, sweeping inside Tolik's guard, attacking with quick thrusting motions, and gliding out before Tolik could riposte.

The ease with which the massive man shrugged off the strikes from his opponent's training sword suggested that the damage reduction enchantments still held, or that Tolik had monstrous damage reduction of his own. The other duelist was closer to Tony's size and looked to be in much better condition, using the "earth-surfing" to conserve their Stamina in an attempt to whittle down their opponent.

Tony scanned the crowd; something seemed off. Other trainees shouted excitedly to each other, "Did you see that? Pay up!" pointing toward the pit and exchanging glowing stones that had to be some sort of currency.

Tolik appeared to be the crowd favorite. Tony focused intently on the fight, falling into old habits from his tournament days.

"A chance to study your opponent in battle must be capitalized on to gain advantage," his Master's words echoed in his head.

Tolik wasn't badly beaten, his breathing was even and his posture was upright. He had been in the ring fight after fight, yet no one had been able to bring him down or unsteady him. The Ashtar he was fighting thought he was in control, but Tolik's blocks and feigned telegraphing was what truly dictated the pace of the fight.

"That son of a bitch isn't stuck in there, he's farming experience from the other trainees," Tony commented. Tony looked at the nameplate again.

"Level: 6*"

What was the asterisk for?

Tolik and the Ashtar were the same level, most of the other trainees that had been in the ring prior were between levels four and six. How was he beating them so badly without taking equal damage?

A hand latched around Tony's shoulder like a vice, snapping him out of the thought. "You're next." a gruff voice said in his ear as the hand lurched him toward the pit's entry.

The crowd seemed to part in front of him and whoever was doing the manhandling. Tony finally got his footing back and pried the hand off his shoulder.

"I'm going, don't have to push," he said, not looking at whoever had brought him here and marching to the rack of training weapons.

He glanced over at the pit as cheers erupted from the crowd. Tolik had won, again, the haft of a broken training spear resting across the back of his incapacitated foe. Tony groped around the training weapons as he continued to watch. Tolik didn't gloat or try to rile the crowd; he instead waited patiently for the next match, regaining what little stamina was lost during the fight.

A wooden gladius hilt found its way into Tony's grip, and he retrieved the weapon. An icon appeared under his HP, Stamina, and Mana bars, silhouettes that telescoped into each other. He focused on it.

Ancestral Heritage: Double-Edged Swords – Accuracy and Damage with Double-Edged Swords is increased by 10%. Defense Rating Increased by 20%

"CAN ANYONE DETHRONE THE CURRENT CHAMPION OF THE GAUNTLET? LET'S FIND OUT IF ANTONIOUS KING IS UP TO THE TASK! BETTING RESOLVES AT THE SECOND BELL!" an Air-Aspected Ashtar announcer shouted, an innate talent magnifying the volume of his voice to pierce the roar of the crowd.

"That's you, Antonious," the gruff voice said again.

Tony nearly jumped out of his skin and whipped around in surprise. The man looking back at him was well-muscled, armed to the teeth, and covered head to toe in plate armor. A pair of pale-blue eyes glared back at him. Why anyone would need so many weapons, Tony could not guess. "Time to get in there. He's not as tired as he looks, so stay sharp," the giant said, his azure eyes gleaming with expectation.

"I know he's not. Just not sure how I'm supposed to close a five-level gap," Tony said.

The not so subtle hint of sarcasm was not lost on the armored titan.

"You'll figure it out!" the man bellowed over the din of the crowd.

Tony walked into the ring, his mouth dried out, and his heart pounding against his ribs. He wasn't ready for this, he needed more time to plan, to evaluate, and most importantly, five more levels at least. The battered squire stood from his stool and approached Tony, dried dirt kicking up in dust clouds around his massive boots.

"Hello, friend. I am Tolik, let's have a good match, yes?" he said, extending his hand to shake.
Tony nodded, ignoring the hand. He had been sucker-punched far too many times at the beginning of a match to trust the gesture. "Yeah, sure." He tested the balance of the wooden sword, it was no fencing foil or saber, but it would work.

Tolik took a few steps back and retrieved his broken spear from the sand and tensed his legs. A surge of adrenaline slammed through Tony's veins. An icon of two crossed swords appeared to the left of his "Ancestral Heritage" buff.

> You are in Combat

A brass bell chimed twice, and Tolik rushed at him with surprising speed. The haft of the spear over his head careened toward Tony in a vicious downward strike, carrying the brute's weight and momentum behind it.

Tony lurched to the right; the wind gusted past him as he dodged by a hair's breadth. The horizontal follow-up caught Tony in the ribs and off guard, sending him sprawling. The crowd "oohed" and sucked wind as a collective. Tony sprung to his feet nearly immediately, then fell to one knee, pain blossoming and spreading through his side. Tolik chuckled from where he stood, a good five meters from where Tony had been standing.

There's no way this guy is level six, he thought.

"That is good, Antonious, the last one I got with that one didn't get back up. You have spirit!"

Tony's retort caught in his chest. Breathing hurt, at least one of his ribs was cracked. He would have to get clever if he wasn't going to get clobbered in the first minute of the match. He shook his head to clear it and focused. He hated it when people called him by his full name, especially when it came from some arrogant over-leveled jackass. Tony slammed his fist into the ground and was pleasantly surprised when a small crater formed under it.

The traits taken from the headset sync translated to more than just boosted Attributes. Summers packed with martial arts tournaments at his father's discretion had pitted him against a smattering of opponents, stronger, bigger, faster, more experienced. He was able to win, he *wanted* to win, he *needed* to win.

The primal part of Tony's brain kicked into overdrive. That part of his brain determined that he could handle taking a couple of hits to evaluate Tolik's fighting patterns. He endured two more charges, once dodging to the left that ended the same way as the first, he tried dodging back as well but Tolik just stepped in after the haft slammed into the dirt and spun in to slam him across the gut with it. Tony coughed and sputtered, spit and a little bit of bile came up splattering into the dirt. A smirk crept across his face.

He figured it out, how to counter his opponent.

Tolik charged him again, this time with the spear pointed at Tony, and held tight against his massive frame. Against his own instinct and to Tolik's delight, Tony stood his ground, gladius gripped firmly in both hands. As the pole entered Tony's guard, he shifted his sword to the right until the blade was parallel with his shoulder. A small movement that sent the spear harmlessly past him.

Tony used the giant's momentum against him, like a matador to a bull, and spun to his outside, slashing out with the training weapon as Tolik's bulk came back into view. The wooden sword smashed against Tolik's back and caused him to stagger forward, interrupting the horizontal counterattack and sending the giant off balance.

Tony danced back from Tolik's second attempt at a follow-up attack. A sloppy wide swing that Tony knew better than to disregard as a desperate attempt to bait him inside Tolik's reach. The behemoth rocketed from the ground like a freight train at Tony.

The splintering remains of the spear scraped against the dirt and gravel of the pit. Tolik aimed the vicious uppercut at the underside of Tony's chin.

Tony sidestepped again like he had before and exactly how Tolik expected. Time dilated as Tony's eyes darted back and forth over his opponent. The tears in Tolik's tunic revealed tensing muscles along the sides of his torso; Tony memorized the way the muscles flexed and stretched. The pattern was simple, vertical attacks that were too risky to parry followed by devastating horizontal attacks.

Brutal and effective.

Tony raised his short sword, blade out, and leaned into it. He may not be the immovable object to Tolik's unstoppable force, but he needed to stop the second attack.

Splinters of wood exploded out from the two weapons as they collided. In the split second that Tolik looked down at the ruined spear in shock, Tony leaped and planted a flying knee into the side of his head, sending him crashing to the ground. Tony stood at the ready, the remaining half of a wooden sword in his hand.

Tolik didn't stir. Tony could see that he was still breathing.

The bells chimed, and the crowd exploded with noise. Tony's eyes went wide as his interface flooded with experience notifications.

> You have ended Tolik's KO Spree. You are rewarded with Bonus Experience.
> You have received 20% of a Player's wagered Experience.

The second notification repeated more times than Tony could count without scrolling through them. People could bet experience? How much XP had Tolik farmed out from winning against other starting characters? Were the crystals changing hands in the crowd XP?

The walking arsenal from earlier signaled the announcer by drawing a line across his neck.

"SQUIRES, THE FIGHTING PITS ARE NOW CLOSED! PLEASE, RETURN TO YOUR ASCENDANT TRAINERS FOR FURTHER INSTRUCTION!"

Tony didn't have one of those yet, so he took a moment to open his character sheet and find out just how much XP he had gained.

Side Quest Completed: King of the Ring

XP: 15

Wagered XP Collected x 17

XP: 85

You have met an XP Milestone! 100 Down, Millions to Go

You have met an XP Threshold, speak with your Ascendant Trainer!

And that, Tony thought, *is how you skip the tutorial.*

Chapter V: User Error

Tony flicked through the smattering of notifications that popped up as quickly as he could. *How annoying,* he thought.

A majority of them were individual experience gain notifications and then there were **all** of the reminder notifications about speaking with his Ascendant Trainer:

You have gained Skill Points!
Speak with your Ascendant Trainer to unlock the Skills Tab!
You have unlocked an Achievement: Under-leveled Overachiever - Defeat an opponent 10 or more levels above yours in honorable combat

Tony took a moment to flick through the various tabs in his character menu now that he had some time to do so. He furrowed his brow and scowled; there was a lot to sort through. *So annoying,* he thought, bypassing the obvious glitch in the achievement.

Under "character," several sub-tabs glistened at him, clamoring for his attention: Overview, Status, Equipment, Attributes, Skills, and Traits. Many of them lacked the emboldening shine of the Overview and Attributes tabs. Tony guessed that this was the system's way of "graying out" options that were unavailable.

Besides the main "Character" tab, the Social, Quests, and Settings tabs gleamed, fully accessible to him. Focusing on a specific notification would bring up the associated menu, at least it had when Tony focused on notifications regarding quests. When Tony focused on "Usurp the Mad King," the "Current Quests" menu had popped up. He tried focusing on the notification about his skill level-up.

Nothing happened. *C'mon, work with me here.*

He tried again and instead of nothing, the sound of TV static filled his ears along with a booming, authoritarian system voice:

> You do not have access to this Tab.
> Speak with your Ascendant Trainer immediately.

"Great, now the system is on my back," he groaned. Tony looked up from his menus, exasperated, and found he was now face-to-helmeted-face with the plate-wearing walking armory. He made the conscious effort *not* to jump out of his boots. "You ever hear of personal space?" Tony said. He put his hand up to the helmet and pushed, moving away instead of pushing the large man. The desired outcome achieved, Tony was content.

"Are you finished fiddle-fucking around?" the man said, his voice gruffer than a bear with coarse-grade sandpaper for fur, matching the absolute contempt in his piercing eyes.

Tony got a feeling and decided to try something. Sometimes, when someone bullies you and you step up to them they can build some form of respect.

"Only if you're done with being in my face," Tony answered defiantly. A notification, barely visible, popped up in the corner of his vision:

D liked that
Your Social Link with D has increased to Level 1!

The man's eyes did not soften so much as shift, like the same sandpaper bear deciding to adopt a human instead of eating them. "Good. Auren is waiting for us in the launch bay. Let's go." Tony was glad that he had stepped up to D, fairly certain that the increased Social Link level was significant in some way. He'd explore the social menus later.

Tony was positive that if he paused to focus on the notification he was likely to catch the back of a gauntleted hand across the face. Tolik had been able to send him flying and was sure that "D" would be able to do the same several times over.

He ignored the notification and followed the tank-like man out of the training grounds to the next hangar. "Are we going to another launch bay?" Tony asked.

"Yes," D grunted.

"Why?"

"Because we're leaving the flagship," D answered.

"Already?"

"We're going to bring you to another training zone." Tony was about to say something when D cut him off. "I know that you just leveled and that you do not have access to the majority of your menus. As your Ascendant Trainer, I will unlock those for you."

"Oh," Tony muttered. He had hoped that Auren would be his Ascendant Trainer, and D seemed like kind of a jerk.

"Your show in the pits tells me that continuing to train you here would be a waste of my time and of your talent," D explained.

"W-was that a compliment?" Tony asked, flabbergasted.

D rolled his shoulders under the gargantuan gleaming pauldrons and continued down the corridor, refusing to answer. Tony jogged to catch up with a smirk plastered on his face.

Soon enough, Tony and D were standing in front of Auren and a midnight starfighter. The craft was sleek and sharp at the same time and seemed to pull the surrounding light into it, blurring its edges. Tony circled the thing; it reminded him of one of the Naboo fighters from the *Star Wars* prequels.

Auren walked down the plank, his toga replaced by loose-fitting leather pants, banded faulds, and a lamellar breastplate. "Ready to go?" the Lord of Auras asked, a clear note of excitement in his voice.

"Yeah!" said Tony.

The three of them walked up the plank and into the ship. Despite the "stealth fighter" look on the outside, the interior was interestingly arranged. The cockpit was at the front and looked to be a bubble, though the outside showed no such protrusions, upon exiting there was a "deployment" area where seats to strap into were located.

Subtle circular grooves on the floor that matched the size of the seats made Tony wonder if they were ejection seats or if the passengers were the intended payload.

Beyond deployment was a lounging area, what looked like a couple of soda machines and food processors adorned a section of wall near a corner booth, from there was the cargo hold, which was mostly empty, and the plank. There would be room on this ship for maybe three more people beyond Tony, Auren, and D; unless one of them was another D, then maybe just one more.

After exploring the inside of the ship, Tony sat at the booth and scanned through the Social menus. He found the social link page and what he saw shot one of his eyebrows into his hairline.

Auren: Social Link Level: 3 | Acquaintance

D: Social Link Level: 1 | Begrudged Presence

Tolik: Social Link Level: -10 | Hated Enemy*

*Warning: This individual is likely to be hostile toward you

Tony hadn't done anything to Tolik other than to beat him in an *unfair* fight, where Tolik had the advantage. Why would he look at Tony as an enemy?

"Something wrong?" Auren asked, noting Tony's expression.

"Just a weird Social Link thing..." Tony half answered. He wondered if Auren would have any idea what he was talking about.

"Want me to take a look?" the god asked.

> Auren, Lord of Auras has requested to share your Screen
> Accept   Deny

Tony focused on the accept option and Auren walked over to look over his shoulder.

"That is a little strange," Auren noted. Tony dragged his Achievement tab into the shared screen and pointed to "Under-leveled Overachiever."

"That one was a little weird too," Tony noted.

"How so?" Auren asked.

"Well, Tolik was only level six when we fought." Auren opened and closed his mouth, looking for the words to say in answer before D walked in.

"Tony, do you want to see something cool?" he asked.

Tony looked at him and quirked his eyebrow. "Uh, sure I guess."

"This will not hurt, much," D said as he extended his hand out towards Tony and a flash of light erupted from his palm and shot into his eyes, riding the most direct pathway to his brain and then shooting through his entire nervous system.

"What the hell!" Auren shouted at D.

Auren's mouth continued moving, but the sound of his heart pounding in his ears and a high-pitched whine drowned out all other sounds. Tony's body burned from the surface of his skin all the way down to the bone. Information seared itself into the fibers of his entire being and brain. His body was locked, roasting in place.

Tony's eyes flicked to his Status bars, his mana bar was at full and flashing chaotically while his health dropped dangerously by the second. Buffs and debuffs appeared sporadically all over his vision. His skin flashed, flickering between scorched meat and translucent blue, purple, and white scrawling code.

Layers upon layers of symbols that he'd never seen before formed beneath the surface of his skin, lines intersecting with each other, and forming lattice networks. He felt every character.

Tony's HP hit zero and the bar flashed with the same chaotic rhythm of his mana bar. D had killed him.

Is this what dying in VR feels like?

His status bars shattered in the interface as every other symbol that had mounted in his vision detonated, sending him to a black screen in a shower of glass confetti.

Congratulations! Your menus have been unlocked.
You are unconscious.
Wake Time remaining: Unknown
You have unlocked an Achievement: The First One's a Doozy

Chapter VI: No Way Back

"What the? How am I?" Tony grumbled. His head was pounding and his skin prickled like he had been out in the cold for too long and jumped into a scalding shower. Minutes passed before he managed to slump himself against the wall. His eyes shot open when the nape of his neck made contact with the cold steel of the starship's wall.

No way.

His head whirled around taking in the lounge. He had landed on the floor ten feet from where he was standing when D "flashed" him. Tony's vision spun and blurred. He snapped his eyes shut and breathed deeply through his nose before bile threatened to choke him. Tony broke out in a cold sweat, the cool spots adding a "static" sensation to the burning of his skin.

He was still in the game.

This doesn't make any sense! The game should have logged me out when I went under, that's how VRMMOs work! Why am I still here?

His mouth cleared of the breaching vomit, Tony regulated his breathing, taking in cold soothing air through his nose and blowing out a hot acrid breath through his mouth. He was going to need a minute.

"I know that's how your menus were activated, Demnas, but that's not how we do things in the program anymore! There are too many risks!" Auren said in a harsh whisper.

"I'd say the risk was well worth it," D's voice hissed back, "we both agreed that the kid was a natural, and if we're going to take this seriously he needs to be up to speed as soon as possible. Isn't that why you wanted me to train him?" The dull thump of metal punching into leather echoed in Tony's aching head. "I didn't manually open his menus to make him suffer."

"Why then?" Auren demanded, the sound of a hand slapping against metal punctuating the question.

"Because it happened again, Auren. I had the vision again." For a second, Tony thought he heard a pang of fear in D's voice. The tinnitus ringing in his ears corrected that assumption. "If the program is going to have a chance it needs a forerunner. No level 1 Squire just walks into the pit and takes on a specialized opponent. I think Tony's the best shot for that."

Tony cracked the sobering silence that followed, struggling and failing to get to his feet as he and the table he'd braced against crashed to the floor. Spots exploded in his vision and air rushed out of his lungs.

"Little help?" he groaned. Something impacted his chest and a warm sensation spread over him, easing the fraying static on his skin and clearing away the fog in his head. As his vision cleared, Tony noted that he was on fire.

"Shit!" he yelled, rolling across the ground, trying to put himself out before he burned to death.

Auren made him pause. "You're... you're not really on fire... it's a... it's a healing spell," he managed to get out between booming laughs. Tony pushed himself up and brushed off his tunic as the "flames" guttered out. His HP, Mana, and Stamina bars were all topped off.

"So what was all that about?" Tony demanded, menacing toward the two gods.

"What are you talking about? The healing..." Auren said, the remnants of laughter still exiting his tone.

"Manually opening my menus? The cryptic bullshit about bad dreams?" Tony practically screamed at them. He threw his arms open, waiting for an answer.

"Tony-" Auren started.

"Impact!" D shouted, cutting off the rest of his words as the starfighter rocked with a booming explosion, throwing Tony back to the floor.

"Strap in now!" D yelled, picking Tony up and flinging him toward the deployment seats.

D blurred from the spot and seemed to reappear in the cockpit at the main controls; Auren slipped into the co-pilot's seat a nanosecond later.

Tony's vision snapped into laser focus and a flashing box pulled his attention to the status bar; there was a bloodshot eye flashing underneath his stamina bar, which was emptying fast.

Buff Activated: Alarming Reflexes
Consume Stamina to Heighten Reflexes, Movement Speed, and Coordination for a limited time. Will use HP when Stamina is unavailable.

Tony burned the waning Stamina Points and five percent of his HP to slam himself into a seat, fasten the safety harness over his chest, and put on the full helmet that dropped into his lap.

Crash Helmet: This one-time armor piece will prevent death via cranial trauma one time
Note: Will not prevent death from blood loss or internal hemorrhaging

D and Auren worked in near silence; the only sounds Tony heard were coming from the now-whining engines of the craft, the furious depression of triggers, the resulting blasts, and the rapid-fire tapping of fingers on the glass.

Tony could see blossoms of flame through a small viewport against a sickly orange starscape. Viridian stars and neon planets flashed by as the fighter weaved through the chaos of the dogfight.

The pair of deities shot ship after ship out of the stars; they were going to make it.

"Brace!" D shouted.

The ship rocked again as a hole ripped open in the hull. The vacuum of space tore at the inside of the fighter, dumping tables, boxes, and weapons into the viridian expanse.

I'm out of here, Tony thought. This was all too much.

Tony pulled up his menu and focused on the settings tab, then the "Game" sub-tab.

His heart stopped.

There was no "Log Out" option, no "Exit Game," no "Safe to Remove Headset" no way out. Gambit Games would not have shipped a headset, even a beta unit, that could not be removed safely from the options screens. He had to be missing something. Right?

Tony searched frantically as the temperature in the ship rose sharply. Flames licked against the ship's hull as it entered the atmosphere.

There had to be something in the options that would get him out of here. His eyes hovered over the "Respawn" option, but it wasn't available.

> Respawn: Returns you to your chambers aboard the
> Haght'anak*
> *The destination is contested

Tony's heart plummeted into his gut. He had no idea what day it was, and he was effectively stuck in the game until he could reach someone in support at Gambit Games. Worse than that, he was going to miss work. He caught a flash of red out of the newly formed and still-smoldering hole in the hull and then green as the ship leveled off, upside-down.

"Is that grass?" he wondered aloud as the fighter slammed into the ground beneath it. His health bar dropped by twenty percent at the first impact, the safety harness cut into his collarbone, and Tony clenched his jaw. Another ten percent of his HP sloughed off as Tony was slammed around viciously in his seat.

The ship ground to a halt on a field of blue-green grass, a fifty-foot furrow dug in the earth from the point of impact. A blaze of gold flame filled the cabin as Auren activated his Battle Aura, burning away the mangled safety harness and, coincidentally, restoring five percent of Tony's missing health. "What happened?" Tony asked as he grappled with the clasp of his harness.

D strode into the cabin, neon-blue fluid streaming off of his armor. "Deep space scan found the ship. It's cloaked from local scans due to the metal it... Well, it was made out of. Someone must have tampered with the long-range cloaking systems before we left."

"I mean, how did we get here? Who shot us down?" Tony stated. With a click, the clasp over his chest released and he fell from the "ceiling" of the craft to the deck.

"Scout ships of the Cadre of Judgement. They were waiting for us," D answered. Tony opened his mouth to ask more questions, but Auren beat him to it.

"Waiting for us? How-"

"Someone must have told them we were coming here. Since Sparky here is in the program, he would have respawned back on the flagship, but that wouldn't have kept us away. There's something else going on here."

Tony piped up, interrupting the two gods. "Okay, first off 'Sparky?' I'm putting the kibosh on that right now. Second, all of that means that you have a mole on the ship that fed Ignacious, or at least their handler, our flight path which is how they got the drop on us from where we jumped into the system, that is, if I'm guessing all of this right."

He looked back and forth between the two. "I also had the option to respawn to the ship but it's contested right now."

D's head snapped up. "We need to do something now. The ship isn't going to make it back any time soon and the kid isn't going to make it out here by himself," he spat at Auren.

Auren cupped his chin in his fist. The two of them continued to exchange words talking mostly as though Tony weren't even there, and if he was, it was about how much of an inconvenience he was at present.

Tony ignored the two gods and acknowledged his notifications. His Endurance, Wisdom, and Wits had all increased by one point and the skill menu had been unlocked.

Tony had a little time and ten Skill Points to spend; it would probably be better to spend them now rather than later. Stranded on a foreign planet with who knows what on the surface, Melee, Athletics, and Survival were straightforward and obvious choices.

Fortitude: This skill represents training in physical resistance. Put points in this skill to passively increase resistance to: Damage, Poison, Disease, Exertion, and Extreme Climate by 1% per Skill Point.
Occult: This skill represents training in the mystical and paranormal. Put points in this skill to increase understanding of Gods, Spirits, Demons, Ghosts, and Essence.

Tony allocated three points into his Melee and Awareness skills, and one point each into his Occult, Survival, Fortitude, and Athletics Skills.

A metallic skittering brought Tony's attention out of his menus. He strained his hearing and heard it again, on the outside of the wreckage, and moving toward the gash in the hull.

D groaned and thrust his hand toward Tony. When a pair of notifications popped up, he double-checked his traits and was delighted at an extra two points in Melee from his Ancestor Heritage Bonus.

You have inherited a Squire Talent! Summon Blade: Create an Essence-Constructed Weapon Cost: 50 Mana Duration: Until Released
You have unlocked an Achievement: Initiate (Melee) Achieve a total Skill Rank of (5) in Melee)

"You're gonna need that," D growled.

"Huh? Why?" he answered, looking around.

D jerked an armored thumb over his shoulder in the direction of the tear in the hull at the biggest spider Tony had ever seen in his life. Its body was the size of an inner tube and each of its legs was easily eight feet long.

"Spiders. It had to be a fucking spider planet."

Chapter VII: Input Overload

The blazing white Essence Blade sprang into Tony's waiting grip just in time for him to meet the maw of the first spider surging through the breach to devour him. The phantom blade sank into the arachnid's flesh past its mandibles, bypassing the kevlar-like chitin. A sickening squelch and brilliant-yellow ichor splashed onto the steel floor. Tony wretched at the smell.

An instant after the life fluid of the spider settled it blackened, hardening around Tony's feet. He wrenched his legs from the spot and stepped back.

Great, Xenomorph spiders, minus the acid, plus being stuck in place.

The shrill hiss of another horse-sized spider snapped Tony back to his senses. The hole in the hull was big enough for maybe three of the beasts to get through at a time if they squeezed together. The things seemed to not consider that approach as one spider at a time would approach the edge of the breach and lunge at him from there.

"When enemies approach you from the same direction in one after the other, you have two options; you rush to meet the advance and disrupt the flow or you leave. There is no in-between that results in victory,"

The words of his Historical Eastern Martial Arts instructor, Ser Seavey, echoed in his head.

Is the game reading my mind to give in-game reminders or did I remember that on my own? Tony thought.

Another massive spider felled, he looked over to Auren and D. They watched as if evaluating him instead of moving to join him.

"A little help?" Tony said.

D continued to stare at him from the slit of his helmet and Auren closed his eyes before shrugging at him and smiling. "Wouldn't want you to miss out on XP! You've got this."

Tony growled and held the Essence Blade in both hands; most games applied a bonus to Strength-based damage when a weapon was used two-handed.

The spectral gladius fit perfectly in his grip despite the Roman short sword design, and though weightless, was perfectly balanced. He tensed his core and felt the ripple of his muscles activating as he readied to meet the wave of arachnids.

As soon as the many-eyed head of one was fully in view Tony dashed forward and leaped up through the breach, separating the head from the thorax. His feet hit the hull and the white of the Essence Blade flashed through the surprised arachnids waiting for their turn to jump through the hole.

Tony's heart pounded in his ears as he looked out over the horde of them. The sea of spiders did not reach the horizon, but he couldn't see the back of them as they poured through the trees.

His moment of hesitation granted the spiders the time they needed to regroup. At the screech of one *massive* spider toward the middle of the swarm, they charged, a never-ending swarm of angry clicking mandibles and spear-like legs.

Tony's Health and Stamina bars fluctuated wildly as he fought to maintain space in the flood of arachnids. Sometimes he got lucky enough to carve off a leg or two before they reached him, others he would feel the white-hot scoring lines of freshly drawn blood across his back or his arms or legs before he had a chance to react.

This was not the "power-leveling" experience Tony had been expecting. He blocked out all of the XP gain notifications after he lost count of how many spiders he had slain just trying not to be forced back into the ship.

The solidified ichor coating the bodies behind and to Tony's sides made a bottleneck for the swarm to approach from, but also prevented any sort of retreat.

Striking down three spiders attacking him in unison with a well-timed sweeping counter slash as he had been at critical HP jumping him up a level had saved him. The HP gain equal to the difference of his total pool pulled him out of the red and allowed him to keep fighting.

I bet picking a couple of talents would make this a lot easier, Tony mused, hand pressed against the "flat" of his Essence Blade, pushing against the clicking mandibles of one of the "Rally Spiders." These larger spiders would screech to signal their cluster of the swarm to advance on him, and would fight him solo at the end of a "wave."

Tony took advantage of the momentary "lull" in dueling the Rally Spider to address his status screen. He had gained three levels, a passive ability called "Berserker's Stance", and two talent points to spend.

Berserker's Stance: Killing an enemy that yields XP will increase Stamina Regeneration by 2%
(to a maximum of 10% bonus Regeneration)
Cost: None   Duration: Indefinite

Tony ducked his head to the left, narrowly avoiding one of the Rally's razor-sharp forelegs and wrenched the edges of his blade across the corners of its screeching maw. The Rally reared back, continuing to wail in agony, and Tony surged forward to bury half of his blade into its eyes. The larger spider seized once and collapsed.

Tony knew that the next wave was coming soon and he would have to make his choices quickly. He selected an upgrade to the inherited Essence Blade talent called "Life-Biting Essence."

Summon Blade: Create an Essence Constructed Weapon
Cost: 50 Mana   Duration: Until Released
Life-Biting Essence: Essence Weapon gains 20% Life Drain

The second talent that jumped out at Tony as most useful was "Pommel Strike." He had always avoided the "entry-level" control effects like what Pommel Strike offered in other games, but when he looked at the web of talents, it seemed that there would be upgrades down the line.

Tony confirmed the selection and hoped that the upgrades would scale with the enemies he faced. Having a talent that would stun an enemy and deal minimal damage wouldn't do a whole lot if enemies became immune to stunning effects.

Pommel Strike: Deal minimal damage to an enemy by attacking with the pommel of your weapon to stun them for 2 seconds.
Cost: 10 Mana   Cooldown: 5 seconds

Selections made and progress reviewed, Tony was delighted to see that he had nearly reached level five. He would be able to select a specialization soon and he was eager to get out of the "Squire" class and talents to see what else was in store for him.

Keeping his stance ready, Tony couldn't help but notice that the swarm had stopped advancing. He stood alone on top of the ruined starship as an eerie silence settled in.

You have been challenged by the Swarm Alpha
You have 2 (minutes) to proceed to the Dueling Grounds

Tony moved to hop down from the ship. He couldn't see where the Alpha was, but he noticed that the swarm had fanned out around the ship to form a large ring.

"Hold on a second," Auren's voice piped up from below. Tony climbed over the rigid carcasses of the fallen spiders between him and the breach and looked through at the God. Tony felt his jaw clench as he looked at both Auren and D. Neither of them had moved from the spot throughout the entire fight.

"Good job!" Auren said, a perfect smile brimming across his face. As he extended an enthusiastic thumbs up in Tony's direction, he noticed a buff icon appear under his status bars.

Burning Essence: +20 Fire Damage to Essence-Based Attacks
Duration: 20 Minutes   Conditions: Does Not Persist Through Death

Ominous, Tony thought.

"Thanks, I guess," he muttered before stepping off of the ship.

"He's advancing quickly," D said to Auren once the sounds of combat rang out.

"Yes, he is. Glad to see one of the initiates *really* getting after it," Auren answered proudly.

D slugged him in the shoulder, his tone leaden. "If he keeps going at this rate Ignacious is going to notice. That's a Swarm Alpha out there."

"None of the other initiates beat their first boss until after they were level ten, did they?" Auren asked, the swelling pride in his chest deflated like a balloon stuck with a needle.

"Nope," D answered.

"So-" Auren started before the bloodcurdling scream of a dying elite spider filled the cabin.

Tony landed on the blue-green grass of the rolling plain the ship came to rest in. The ring of spiders all shifted as one to look at him and Tony felt his eyebrows hit his hairline when those in the front raised their forelegs in an X in front of their bodies. The swarm parted in front of Tony and he swore that if his eyebrows went any higher they'd shoot off of his face.

Instead of pockmarking the earth with puncturing limbs and tremendous size, the Alpha seemed to glide over the earth, her lower four spider legs carrying the rest of her off the ground.

Tony *hated* spiders, but *she* was attractive. She wore a kimono clearly woven from spider silk, and with the exception of a visible set of extra eyes, three-inch claws extending from her fingers, and the eight spider legs protruding from her lower back, she appeared very human. Her glowing green eyes settled on Tony after looking him up and down. In contrast to her cascades of black hair, they were striking.

The splashes of "skin" that Tony could see were bright red and he could see the shapes of chitin plates among her very prominent curves through the kimono.

She spoke first in a series of hisses and rhythmic clicks of the arachnid appendages, to which Tony said, "What?"

She blinked rapidly at him after that and worked her jaw, seeming to chew on the word that she heard and then spoke again, slowly.

"Iss it youu who hass sslain myy kinn?" Her voice was a pleasant alto, and despite the odd tempo of her speech, Tony understood her well enough.

"It was," he admitted, relaxing his stance only slightly. Her jaws worked the words over again.

To his unending surprise, the spider-woman bowed to him, the set of eyes on her forehead locking with his. "Youu arrre a ssskilled warrriorrr," she said.

It seemed that her skill with the English language was improving the more of it that she heard.

So, she's wearing a kimono, challenged me to single combat, is complimenting my skill as a warrior and none of the more base spiders are going to engage, Tony recounted.

He returned the bow, trying to maintain eye contact with both sets of eyes at once. "Your brood is a fearsome one. You do me a great honor," he answered. Tony maintained the bow and the woman gestured at him to stand.

Her jaw continued to work for another minute before Tony saw her swallow.

The voice that poured out of her caressed Tony's ears like silken sheets. "We have not encountered a one like you before. As ample as my curiosity is, the time for pleasantries has passed." A look of hard focus came across her unlined face as chitin spread across her visible skin.

The woman's claws retracted as she removed the kimono and lowered to her two human legs; she was covered nearly head to toe in chitinous plating.

Tony admired this character's design, it would have been easy for Gambit to leave the stereotypical "cleavage window" in her armor and to have her speak the same language as a player right away. The devs could have had her try to seduce them only to murder them like a "black widow," but that wasn't who this woman was. She was a warrior.

"Wait a moment, please," Tony said, extending his left hand, palm up toward the woman.

She eyed him expectantly.

"It is customary where I trained to exchange names before a duel and to state terms, is this way agreeable to you?" he asked.

She smiled before she spoke, and behind the row of flattened human teeth, Tony could see at least two more rows of serrated, tearing fangs. "This way is pleasing to me. I am Jorogu of the Yokai cluster, second daughter of Queen Semiramis and Master of the Katakana."

All but two of her spider legs retracted into her body. The two legs that remained interlocked and melded together before separating from her body entirely and landing in her waiting hands. The sharpened sides of the legs formed a lethal single-edged blade reinforced by interlocked segments of spider leg that tapered into a handle. Jorogu pressed the flat of the blade to her lips and swung the blade down, its edge millimeters from the ground.

Tony swallowed hard; he was in for a tough fight.

"I am Antonious King, Squire of the Ascendants, final son of my line, student of battle, walker of the path of self."

Man, my accolades suck, he thought.

"The terms," she spoke, "to the satisfaction, my physician will call for staying of blades should one of us be grievously wounded, as to preserve both our lines. Do you accept?"

Tony nodded. He had been hoping that the duel would be to first blood. Jorogu was a warrior through and through; duels to first blood had been looked at as cowardly early on in the history of the "sport," but was still the common term in most media. He had to give Gambit credit for historical accuracy at the least.

Another spider stepped out from the swarm, this one in a state of metamorphosis between the spiders Tony had been fighting already and Jorogu, maintaining a spider's body, but possessing the upper body of a woman. Tony was grateful that this new spider saw fit to wear clothes on her upper half.

"This is Ama. She will check your vitals and then my own so that she may monitor them." Ama started to move toward Tony before he protested.

Man, how do I say this without sounding like a dick?

"Jorogu, I take you as an honorable one. Do I have your word as a warrior that Ama will not interfere with our duel? That I would be protected from sabotage?"

The spider-woman smirked. "You are a cautious one. Mother always said that the cautious warrior was the sure one. I swear on my blade that she will not interfere with you or convey information that would give an unfair advantage." Tony lowered his blade and nodded at Ama, whose human half was fair-skinned, emerald-eyed, with blood-red hair pinned up in elaborate loops connected to a bun. She advanced toward him again and lowered her spider body to be eye level with Tony.

He felt his pulse quicken as she placed her hands on either side of his face. Her primary set of eyes, resting just above the bridge of a delicate nose locked with his as the second set on her forehead scanned over him in entirety. "I must sample to monitor. Is this okay?" she asked quietly, her voice an octave higher than Jorogu's, but with the same cascading tone.

"Uh, yeah. Okay," Tony answered, his cheeks warming under her touch. He braced, expecting to feel a prick or a cut on his cheek.

Instead, he felt surprisingly soft lips press against his and a tongue flick out to gently caress and explore the inside of his mouth.

Tony sank into the embrace, all of the tension and fatigue of combat leaving him in a wave of comfort. Ama let out a surprised squeak and pulled back as Tony kissed back on instinct.

"Oh! Uh, I'm sorry. Bad habit," Tony explained in a hurry.

Ama nodded and swallowed before walking over to Jorogu and replicating the procedure. "I have harmonized your life essences with my own and will call for a stay of blades if one is too injured to continue," she announced.

"On your count then," Tony announced, taking in Jorogu's stance. The tip of her sword remained close to the ground, edge pointing in toward her center.

She's either incredibly fast, or she's going to parry with the back of the sword and riposte. There's probably critical damage on ripostes. Which way is she coming? he thought.

"Begin!" Jorogu shouted.

It turned out that the answer to Tony's internal question was "yes." Jorogu launched herself at Tony like a shot from a cannon. Tony put his sword up between them and just before the blades clashed she disappeared.

Tony swung to the left on instinct and brought his sword down in a powerful overhead arc; Jorogu's parry lifted him three feet off the ground.

Tony's eyes opened and he realized that they had closed at the tremendous crash of essence on chitin. Jorogu was gone again.

Tony looked up just in time to see her careening down at him, sword extended. With no solid ground to brace against or pivot on, Tony turned his essence blade flat and braced his left forearm against it. Jorogu's thrust slammed his hands into his chest and gut. Ten percent of his HP, gone, from a blocked attack.

The wind knocked out of him, Tony slammed into the ground. His lungs burned and his vision blurred, down thirty percent.

Instincts blaring in alarm, Tony rolled to the right. Not even a second later, the sound of a sword crashing through the earth where he had just been rung out.

Come on! Get it together! He closed his eyes tight for a half-second and snapped them open, the world coming into sharp focus. He had lost his grip on the Essence Blade, but a ring of burning white essence around his right wrist told him that the talent hadn't deactivated.

Jorogu twisted her blade in the earth, edge pointed at Tony, and carved it out, sending shrapnel flying at him. He flexed his grip and sliced at the debris.

The blade returned to form as he slashed, carving through the larger chunks and sending the lesser ones harmlessly aside. Jorogu was upon him again, her whole body parallel to the ground and just inches from it. She contorted and twisted, slashing up at him from an angle.

In the heartbeat between the meeting of blades Tony saw the pattern; he just needed to figure out how to turn it on the spider-woman. Unlike the fight with Tolik, he couldn't take hits and go through the pattern until he figured it out. Jorogu dealt too much damage, the duel would be called in her favor if he did.

It's a risk, but I have to do it now!

Tony released his grip on the Essence Blade, reverting it back to the ring of light and weaved backward, keeping his feet planted firmly in Jorogu's path. The tip of the arachnid weapon left a shallow cut squarely in the center of Tony's jawline, claiming one percent of his HP.

He felt the woman's body impact his own for a fraction of a second; in the moment of contact, she went rigid. Tony could tell she would hop back from him, startled from the bizarre impact. He pushed out into a deep lunge and Tony's left knee caught the back of one of Jorogu's legs.

Tony stepped through the lunge and leaped at the spider-woman. Toppling and off-balance, she swung her weapon to intercept his charge, Tony caught the back of it in his left hand and flexed the grip of his right in the same motion.

"I yield," Jorogu said. The abrupt halt of her weapon and Tony's forward momentum had driven her to the ground with the smoldering tip of his Essence Blade resting against the underside of her chin.

"Stay your blades!" Ama called.

Tony's stare bored into Jorogu's main set of eyes and she released the hilt of her weapon. Tony released his Essence Blade talent and gasped, letting out the breath that he had been holding. He took a step back and held out his hand, Jorogu took it and stood.

"I pity those that you call enemies," she said, maintaining her grip on his hand. "I would have you return to the cluster with my brood to meet Mother."

Tony gulped. "I would uh, definitely love to do that but I would need to check with my mentors before venturing off."

"Then I would grant you my brood's blessing that you may find us again at your leisure. Is this okay?" Tony admired her persistence.

You have received a Side Quest: Courted by the Princess of Blades
Jorogu, Princess of the Arach Empire who you bested in a duel has invited you back to meet the Queen of the cluster. Among the Arach this is a common courting practice after finding a suitable mate. She has offered to bestow a blessing upon you so that you may return.
Quest Objective: Be courted by the Princess or spurn her advances
Reward (Court): Blade Blessing+ | Equipment | Positive Social Link (Arach Empire) Reward (Spurn): Bonus XP | Arachnid Advantage | Positive Social Link (Order of the Pristine)

Tony weighed his options for a moment. Jorogu's were a warrior people and even if being hit on by a spider-woman was a little weird, he preferred it to whatever this 'Order of the Pristine' was. "Yes, I would like to be able to see you again."

In slow but deliberate motion, Jorogu raised Tony's wrist to her mouth and sunk a pair of fangs into it. A warm sensation spread over the skin of his forearm, then through his entire body.

Blessing of Blades: Proficiency with Bladed weapons increased by 35%, Proficiency with Arach weaponry increased by 50%, Poison Resistance increased by 70%

Tony took his arm back and looked. The bite marks had healed into the blackened shape of a sword with four sharpened prongs to make up the guard.

"I want you to have this too," she said, holding her blade out to him. Before Tony could question why she cut him off, "Since I separated these legs from my body and lost the duel, I cannot re-assimilate them. It is only right that you should take it with you."

Tony nodded and took the blade in his hands. It was lighter than he expected and even though he had watched it be made, he was incredibly impressed with the quality. He focused on the item and its description and a flush rose in his cheeks.

Jorogu's Marital Blade	Rarity: Unique (1 of 1)
Durability: 100%	Enchantments: Concealed (Social Link 5)
Slashing Damage: Exceptional	Thrusting Damage: Good
Parry: Good	Riposte Multiplier: 3.75x

"Thank you..." Tony said.

"Well then, I must return with my Brood. I do hope that you will return soon." Jorogu reached out and brushed lightly against the mark left on Tony's arm, then turned on her heel and left, the swarm in tow.

Tony slung the sword over his shoulder and jumped when a set of spider legs popped out, latched onto his shoulder, and held the blade tight to his back.

"Well, that's interesting," he said as he started back toward the downed craft. His feet wouldn't move. "What the?" Tony went to reach for his leg, but his arms wouldn't move either, his torso didn't bend either.

A red debuff pulsed under his status bars:

Gaze of the God-King: He Sees You
All Talents Silenced
All Buffs Dispelled (Permanent bonuses not affected)
Movement Reduced by 100%

Well, Fuck.

Chapter VIII: Oathkeeper

Every bit of effort Tony put into moving sapped him of strength; he was stuck alright. The sky's hue shifted from the murky orange to a blazing gold and pulsed with the words of Ignacious, the Mad King.

"Who is this? A fledgling human who comes to a far-off world in an attempt to gain power? My, what a splash you've made today."

Tony's left foot moved an inch and a buzz of annoyed static crackled across his vision.

"And if you are here, that could only mean that Auren is not far, perhaps in the fighter my scouts shot down? Did he really think that he'd outsmarted me? That taking his little resistance into space would hide them from my notice? He should have known better."

Tony's eyes darted to the crippled starcraft. Auren and D were sitting ducks now. Whatever spell Ignacious was using on Tony to root him in place *probably* wouldn't work on either of them.

Log out, Log out, Log out, Log out, LOG OUT! Tony thought. *Why can't I get out?*

"Ah, so that is how they did it, clever," boomed the sky. "You think this is a game?"

Tony's heart skipped a beat. *No way.*

"This is no game, child, this is your life, a whole new adventure, and wonder, all about to come to a dazzling finale. What do you think?"

His mind went blank. Were Ignacious's words part of his monologue? An anticipatory response to what the player would say? Or had he really been trapped in the "game world"? Tony tried to think outside of the game, to will his arms, the arms resting next to his body on his bed in his shitty little apartment, to move to his head and remove the headset.

Nothing.

"There is no headset to remove, no 'Log Out' function to execute, no escape. Didn't Auren tell you?"

That answers that.

Tony pushed the building melancholy down deep within himself. There would be time to deal with that later, or he would die and it would cease to be his problem. His mind raced; he had to do something. A notification flashed, almost in response to his desperation.

> You have unspent Specialization Points!
> Select a Specialization!

He focused on the notification as Ignacious continued to monologue, assumedly at Auren while Tony was locked down. The notification brought him immediately to the Specialization menu. *That's convenient.*

He had the option of forgoing a Specialization to continue gaining levels in Squire at an advanced rate. Now that more of the Squire Talents were visible, Tony decided against that route.

Squire turned into a hybrid Support/Tank class, which he thought was interesting but didn't see a way to use that to his advantage at the moment.

The route he did decide on was to select an Advanced Class. The Advanced Classes he met the prerequisites for were Duelist, Brawler, and Knight.

Duelist: Utilize overwhelming speed and prowess to dominate single targets

Talents Gained on Selection: Challenge, Critical Lunge

Challenge: Enforce your posture with Mana to engage an enemy in single combat

Effect: Gain 10% Bonus to all combat skills and abilities, these bonuses double against your challenged foe if the duel is interrupted by their allies.

Cost: 30 Mana   Duration: 5 minutes

Cooldown: 120 seconds

Special: If only one foe is in the area, this talent remains active until the duel is resolved

Critical Lunge: Attack your opponent with surprising reach, bypassing their defenses

Effect: Gain 10% additional reach for 1 Melee attack. Critical Chance is increased by 60%

Cost: 15 Mana   Duration: Instant

Cooldown: 10 seconds   Damage: Moderate to Extreme

Talent Synergy: Using this Talent against a Challenged foe increases the Critical Chance to 100%

Special: This Talent may only be activated when using a one-handed weapon.

So that's why Tolik was such a beast, Tony thought.

Duelist seemed like a strong selection, but Tony had the feeling that challenging Ignacious to single combat would just get him killed faster. He swiped the Advanced Class aside with his eyes and moved onto Brawler.

Brawler: Start on the road to savagery by beating the life from your enemies with your bare hands.

Talents Gained on Selection: Knuckle Duster, Primal Fighting

Knuckle Duster: Introduce your enemies to your fist, intimately

Effect: Increase Damage type with Natural Weapons up to 2 categories for 1 Attack

Cost: 5 Mana   Duration: Instant

Cooldown: 3 seconds   Damage: Up to Moderate

Note: When using Knuckle Duster against inanimate objects, damage category increases by another three factors to Extreme

Special: Upon activation, a Brawler may designate a Natural Weapon to receive Knuckle Duster. So long as the Brawler is engaged in combat, the Talent will not dissipate until a blow with the designated weapon is successful.

Primal Fighting: Lose yourself to the fury of combat

Witness the Beginning

Effect: For the duration of Primal Fighting, the Brawler receives the following bonuses: Increased Damage, Increased Damage Resistance, Increased Pain Threshold, Temporary Hit Points, Unlimited Stamina

Cost: 50 Mana, 10% HP   Duration: 5 Minutes

Cooldown: 2 Hours*

Bonuses: Damage 30%, Damage Resistance 30%, Pain Threshold 60%, Temporary Hit Points 40% of Max HP

Note: Cooldown is reduced by a factor of remaining Temporary HP, if any.

Special: For the duration of Primal Fighting, all Brawler Attack Talents have a Cooldown of 0 seconds and may be activated using HP when Mana is depleted.

The bonuses from Primal Fighting were tempting, but limiting his combat to "natural weapons" wouldn't make up for the potential drawbacks and certainly wouldn't get him skyward or do anything *now*. If he lived through this and got to pick up another specialization, Brawler could be a great choice.

Knight: Using honor and steel in equal measure, vanquish those that would oppose you

Talents Gained on Selection: Knight's Charge, Oath

Knight's Charge: Move toward a target or combat unit with extreme velocity

Cost: 20 Mana+   Duration: Instant   Range: Varies

Cooldown: 7 seconds   Damage: Special

Note: A Knight must attack the Target of Knight's Charge when using this Talent

Special: Damage to a target after using Knight's Charge is increased by 150%. A Knight may use Knight's Charge against any visible target, additional Mana will be consumed to fuel the Knight's advance.

Oath: The knight swears to the completion of a task. Until the requirements of the Oath are met the Knight receives Passive Bonuses, once the requirements of the Oath are satisfied the Knight gains additional benefits.

Effect: Gain a 20% Oath bonus to all Attributes related to the Sworn Task, reduce debuff durations by 30%

Cost: None   Duration: Until Completes

Cooldown: None*

Completion Bonuses: 5 Attribute Points, 10 Skill Points, 2 Knight/Paladin/Dread Knight Talent Points

Note: A Knight may only have up to their (Essence) Oaths active at one time and is bound to each independently. Utilize Caution when activating this Talent.

Special: An Oath sworn to resolve a Saga will have its bonuses adjusted to scale with the Saga's Difficulty. Additionally, Oaths sworn as a Knight will persist when Specializing the Knight Class to Paladin or Dread Knight.

Note: Knights who Specialize to Anti-Paladin or Chaos Knight will have their Oaths inverted to Pacts as appropriate.

Despite the incredible strain on his body, Tony felt a smirk cross his lips. Knight seemed to be leading in the direction that he wanted to go to progress through-

His train of thought stopped there for a moment. This *wasn't* a game, this was his life now, and while "Respawn" was an option in the menus he couldn't be sure if that was real or just part of the facade to make him a willing participant in whatever scheme was at play.

Tony brushed those notions aside and jammed them into the bottom of his chest with the despair waiting there. Now was not the time for feelings, now was the time for action, to find a way to win.

Tony confirmed his selection of the Knight Advanced Class. His menus wiped away and a system message boomed through the entirety of his being.

Stand with Honor
Defend the Defenseless
Pursue the Wicked that they may see the error of their ways
Purge the Profane, as their souls are lost
Mourn for the loss of innocence
Be humble in Victory
Above all else
Be Absolute in your Resolve

Tony toppled forward as "Gaze of the God-King" fell off his status bars. He regained his footing and drew Jorogu's Marital Blade from his shoulder, not quite sure how to fight the sky.

The garish gold sky flickered to a violent red. "You are a clever one, child, too clever to let live," Ignacious interrupted. With a boom of thunder, the clouds parted as a barrage of golden light hurtled toward Tony.

He made a mad dash in a serpentine pattern as the ground tore up around him from the assault. If he could move into the trees and far enough away from the downed fighter, D and Auren might have a chance to do something about Ignacious.

If the rest of his body had been able to move again, Tony was sure he would have whiplash as the familiar Gaze of the God-King debuff reappeared under his status bar.

Fuck, Tony thought.

"This is what I was talking about, child. Too clever to let live." The sky returned to the golden hue that Tony was starting to get very sick of seeing.

"Is that really all you've got? One pompous debuff and an orbital laser? Give me a break! You suck at this," Tony challenged; at least his mouth still worked this time. There was no answer from the sky, save for the immense boom that shook the whole planet and singular bolt of divine fury heading straight for Tony's face.

The sound of tearing metal drowned out all other sounds as D carved through the side of the fighter and burst through the hull, intercepting the blast with his armored frame.

Tony blinked.

The blast detonated, devastating the surrounding landscape. For a moment, Tony's mind wandered to Jorogu and her swarm. He hoped that they didn't get caught up in the blast.

When the smoke cleared D was standing in front of Tony, only five percent of his total HP missing from the attack. Tony could see the man shaking.

Why? He took that like a champ, his armor isn't even scorched!

"Can you hear me?" D's voice escaped his helmet, a whisper in Tony's ear.

"Yeah, are you okay? Did he hit you with some crazy debuff?"

"I'm... I'm fine, Antonious. I have to tell you something," D said.

Ignacious did not posture, monologue, or taunt. The Mad God responded with absolute force and fury, sending a blast immeasurably larger hurtling at the armored guardian.

That son of a bitch, he knows exactly how much damage he needs to do to kill him!

"No!" Tony screamed, pulling with all his might against the magic holding him in place. It was useless. He couldn't do anything.

Had he not been rooted to the spot, the concussive force of the blast would have sent him into orbit. Shrapnel tore at his extremities, taking his health down by forty percent, D's health dropped to a singular point, and an indicator appeared below D's Status Bars.

> Martyr's Charge: You have been chosen to live. The Martyr will give their life in the protection of yours. Upon the Martyr's Final Death You will receive boons selected from the Afterlife. Welcome home, Noble Soul.

D turned to look at Tony, half of his face a smoldering mess, the other still covered by the remains of his helmet. "I am Demnas, First of the Ascended. You, Antonious, will be my vengeance. Don't just beat him, kid, kick his ass." His voice did not waver, and the ferocity of his gaze shocked Tony, considering what incredible pain he had to be in.

"I don't... I can't..."

"It's okay, Tony, this is how it had to happen."

A second massive blast whistled toward the pair of them. Demnas turned to face it and let out a roar that shook the entire plane. His body shone white and opaque before unleashing a torrent of scarlet energy, countering Ignacious' attack ultimately. A health bar appeared in the sky.

> Ignacious' Avatar
> Level: ???   HP: 17%
> Status: Silenced, Rooted

Tony felt his teeth grind as the fury welling in his chest threatened to pop the cork on all of the repressed emotions he had bottled up. He knew that keeping all of that shit pent up was going to bite him later, that the toxic "Man Up" and "Real men don't cry" bludgeoned into him by his father would probably kill him someday. He didn't care.

Today was not that day.

Tony's eyes flicked down to where D had been focusing on a pair of glowing white footprints, his last stand. Tony buried the tip of his blade into the ground at his side and knelt. He put his right fist over his heart and reached out with his left hand, leaving it just above the smoldering tracks.

"I swear that I will make Ignacious suffer, that I will become worthy of your vengeance. I'll chase him to the Abyss if I must. Ignacious. Will. Pay," Tony managed past the lump forming in his throat.

Oath's buff icon appeared in Tony's status. He looked up into the sky, to the health bar there, and thought *Target*.

A reticle appeared around the nameplate in his vision and the "In Combat" message flashed in his status bar. Tony stood and drew his weapon from the earth.

"What a waste," Ignacious's voice boomed from the avatar, "to think that Demnas gave his life to save a whelp like you. How disappointing."

"Yeah well fuck you too!"

Tony roared, his anger overtaking his rational thought as he burned eighty percent of his Mana and activated Knight's Charge. Tony launched into the air, rocketing toward the glowing avatar, sword trailing behind him. The blade sang as he bisected the humanoid construct in a spray of golden Essence.

As he plummeted toward the ground, Tony rolled over in the air to be looking back up to the fading gold in the sky and showed it the double freedom rockets. A few feet before impact Tony's descent slowed drastically, the glow of the burning footprints intensifying as he landed.

You have inherited an Artifact!

Name: Pauldron of Vengeance

Rarity: Legendary   Quality: Exceptional

Defense Rating: +20   Slot: Shoulders

Effects: Unknown   Activated Abilities: Unknown

Description: The shattered remains of Demnas's "Nemean Pride" Cuirass, the remaining Lion's Maw will easily grip and secure up to two Large-Size weapons. This piece of armor, with the addition of two leather straps, will function as armor and can be affixed to your left shoulder.

"Ignacious!" Auren's voice boomed in concert with the detonation of the expired starcraft. Auren's Battle Aura traced lines of golden fire into the earth to form a series of intricate seals and sigils. Tony's eyes followed the lines for about five seconds before going wide in shock.

"That's a summoning circle, what are you-"

"IGNACIOUS!" Auren screamed. Rage and magic propelled his voice into the sky, clearing it of all debris and cloud cover. Before Tony could blink the sky was back to its sickly orange hue and the lines of the summoning circle vanished in a puff of white smoke.

"I'm gonna kill him," the God decreed.

Chapter IX: A Different Kind of Knight

Auren's chest heaved with effort as he worked to steady his breathing. Tony was surprised to see him short of breath, but considering the overall gravity of trying to summon another God from their place of power, he couldn't be that surprised. Tony's brain kept cycling over what Ignacious had said. Ascendant: Online was *not* a game and Auren had kept information from him.

As if on cue, Auren looked to Tony with a sheepish expression splashed across his face and opened his mouth to speak.

"No, not right now," Tony growled.

"What?" Auren's surprised tone mirrored the expression on his face.

"I don't want to talk about it." Tony's eyes were locked on the two footprints just a pace in front of him.

It didn't make any sense. Demnas had been so much more powerful than Tony could imagine, how could Tony live up to *that*? Like Auren, Demnas had been a God, which means he should have been capable of going toe to toe with Ignacious.

Tony was level six.

Almost in response to his thoughts, a flurry of notifications appeared.

You have unspent Attribute Points!

You have acquired an Artifact!

A Background is ready to be discovered!

You have unspent Skill Points!

You have activated a Saga!

You Survived a direct assault from Ignacious, the Mad King, Bonus XP has been awarded!

Your Artifact's XP Multiplier has Activated!

You have reached Level 10!

Tony ignored them.

Knowing that this wasn't a game, but that this was his life now, had not changed the system that dictated his progress.

"Why is the system acting like this is still a game when it isn't?" Tony half spat at Auren.

"Err- Well," Auren cleared his throat, regained his composure, and continued, "your body has been fitted with what is called an I.A.A.M. which collects the essence generated by your experiences and victories and turns it into fuel for progression. The I.A.A.M. is what generates muscle mass when you increase your Strength Attribute or conveys knowledge when you increase a skill."

"What does I.A.A.M. stand for?" Tony asked.

"Innate Anima Amplification Module."

"And it's talking to me in game-speak because?"

"Because that is what you respond to best. It amplifies your Anima, your life force. It's subjective. No one else in the program should have the same displays, options, or advancements. Similar, maybe, but not one hundred percent the same," the God explained.

"Hm. Well, upgrade time, I guess," Tony said before calling up his menus.

There was a lot to do.

He had ten attribute points to spend, two more talents to select, another specialization point and twenty skill points to allocate; if that wasn't enough to work through, he would have to look at the artifact he gained and scour his background page to see which one he could find. Before he could do any of that, a red pop-up appeared.

> Saga: "War Against Heaven" has been activated.
> Saga Restrictions: Death in combat against Ignacious, The Mad King, or any of his Elite Subordinates will result in Final Death. Be on your guard, and ensure you are appropriately leveled and geared before taking on The Mad King or his minions!
> Special: Character Progression in combat where Final Death is possible has been increased by 25%

Oh Goodie, hardcore mode. Tony acknowledged and dismissed the notification then opened his character sheet.

Ascendant Online's Attribute System operated on modifiers; any score lower than ten was considered "below average" and gave him penalties. Tony put one point each into Charisma, Wisdom, Strength, Endurance, and Wits. Half of his Attribute Points gone, he had to be careful with how he proceeded. He had no negative modifiers, and if he was going to continue through the Knight specialization and kill Ignacious in single combat, he was going to need to improve leaps and bounds in the Attributes that would keep him alive.

The talents that he had selected earlier put him in an interesting position. Tony could go for a "Glass Cannon" build, try to dish out more damage than his enemies could as fast as possible, but that was easily countered by magical defenses or second wind Talents.

The "Life-Biting Essence" upgrade to his Essence Blade talent did reward high damage output, however, if he was going to be hunted down by Ignacious's flunkies they would be sure to have countermeasures in place.

The silver lining of being hunted across the stars by the Cadre of Judgement meant he'd have plenty of opportunity to abuse the additional XP gain, as long as he didn't die. Tony put one point into Spirit, another two points into Strength, and two points into Dexterity.

You have unspent Specialization Points!

With a groan, Tony flicked over to the specialization screen and furrowed his brow. The Knight tree contained what would be expected, upgrades to his Oath and Knight's Charge Abilities, talents focused on mounted combat, leadership and squad tactic boosts, *blah blah blah.*

What surprised him was a pair of glimmering clusters branching off from the Knight tree. On the left was the Paladin Advanced Specialization, bonuses to Charisma, powerful healing spells, abilities to smite the dead and unholy, again, the typical.

This seems a little early to advance the specialization, he thought.

To the right was the "Dread Knight" Advanced Specialization. Tony let out a low whistle as he perused the talents. Dread Knights looked like "Spell Blades: Heavy Metal edition."

Ranged Melee attack talents, bonus damage at low HP, and second wind talents, it was everything he wanted. The icing on the cake was the talent close to the end of the blade Dread Knight tree called "Ichor-Seeking Blade"

Ichor-Seeking Blade	Dread Knight Advanced Talent
Cost: None	Duration: Permanent
Effect: Gain 30% Bonus Damage to Essence Constructs and Divine Beings	
Special: Dealing deathblows to Divine beings will inflict Final Death upon them	
Note: Social Links with Essence Constructs and Divine beings will fall by 3 Ranks upon purchase of this Talent	

Without a second thought, Tony dumped the Specialization Point into Dread Knight, gaining immediate access to the talents "Summon Dreadblade" and "Invincible Will."

Summon Dreadblade: The Dreadblade is a manifestation of the Dread Knight's soul	
Cost: 30 Lore	Duration: N/A
Cooldown: Special*	Properties: Astral, Soulbound
Cooldown: Upon destruction or loss of their soul weapon, a Dread Knight must sacrifice 10% of his total HP as an additional cost to cast "Summon Dreadblade."	
Astral: The Dreadblade can interact with immaterial entities Soulbound: No other beings can wield the Dreadblade without suffering tremendous penalties.	

The Dreadblade would replace his Essence weapon as a talent. Tony was okay with that. Worst case, the Marital Blade was still intact and a formidable weapon.

Invincible Will: Channel your indomitable resolve to negate a single crowd-control effect. You cannot be affected by the same effect for 30 seconds.

Cost: 10 Lore	Duration: 30 seconds

Note: This Talent is ineffective against physical restraints

That would have been useful earlier.

Selections confirmed, he focused on the "Skills" sub-menu. A notification flashed angrily at him and prevented his access.

Your Background is in the Immediate Area!
Background: Sprit-Tied Pet

You Have been assigned a Familiar Quest!
Man's Best Friend
Objective: Rescue your Familiar
Rewards: Familiar, XP, Familiar Equipment
Conditions: Failure to complete the Familiar Quest within the allotted time will result in the loss of your Familiar
Background* (Effect of War Against Heaven Saga)

Tony's throat slammed shut as his heartbeat slammed in his temples. "Max?" he croaked.

Chapter X: Soulbound

This chapter of Ascendant Online is written in memory of my best friend, Maximus. Maximus was with me for nine years and was simply put, the best dog I've ever had. There isn't a day that goes by that I don't miss you.

His blood turned to ice. "Max... Maximus..." Tony whispered past the lump in his throat.

Taking the Dread Knight Advanced Specialization increased his Strength, Stamina, and Spirit by five points each. He'd have to check his sheet later; there was a thirty-minute time limit ticking down in the corner of his vision and an arrow pointing him South.

Tony sprinted past Auren and ran until his stamina bar flashed red. He had never run so fast for so long in his life. His breath came in ragged gasps as his Stamina bar flashed red, nearly empty. He could slow to a quick jog to replenish the bar, and while he grappled with the fact that his current state of being was just that and not a game, his body still responded to the "rules" set by the game.

When his stamina ran close to empty, he struggled for breath and could not run. As soon as it was full, he could run full out with no penalty.

After fifteen minutes had ticked down, the arrow faded and blew out into a dome in his vision.

He was in the quest area and would need to find his pet quickly. Tony took a frantic glance at his surroundings to gain some bearing on where he was.

The direction the quest indicator had taken him was in the same direction that Jorogu's brood had gone. The pathways in the borderlands between the plain they'd crashed in and forest the brood retreated to were well-traveled. He hoped this would make finding his dog easier.

Patches of dense forestation smattered the landscape like a Rorschach test. There was no "easy" way for him to determine which thicket he would find his Familiar in. He'd have to search them all.

As the seconds raced by, a sweat broke out across Tony's back and his breath came in frantic shallow gasps. Max had been the best thing that happened to Tony. His father had used the "I'll get you a puppy if you win" tactic to motivate him at the state-level martial arts tournament and held it over him until he placed first at nationals. Tony had refused to compete in the international competition until his father showed him the adoption papers for the mixed breed puppy he'd picked out online.

Tony's heart raced, threatening to escape his chest. If Maximus was really here and could be saved, he'd do anything to rescue him.

He crashed through the underbrush, patch to patch searching for signs of life. Searching for *anything* that would point him in the right direction.

Ten more minutes passed.

Anxiety turned to frustration, then to fury as he ran madly through the brush when he heard it: a small bark, followed by the gibbering of coyotes. Reacting to his senses, Tony wheeled to the left, toward an unexplored thatch of forest, and sprinted. He burst through brush and branches into a scattered clearing where a pack of six coyotes stared hungrily at their prey.

Standing there, battered and dirty, as though plucked from memory, was Maximus. Stout and auburn-furred, the small dog bared his teeth at the pack of predators, backed into a corner, surrounded. Two of the small wolves turned and snarled at Tony, showing gnarled yellow fangs that matched their hungry eyes.

They were animals, beasts that couldn't be reasoned with. One of them leaped at him as another nipped at the defiant pup. Blood boiling in his veins, Tony acted with a roar and without thought, seizing the beast by its open jaw. He twisted and opened up his hips, swinging it into an adjacent tree.

Dried bark and bloodied fur flew with the monster as he released it and rounded on the rest. In a flurry of punches and kicks, Tony got between the pack and his dog. Despite his recent advancements, Tony's Health Bar was down by about forty percent and ticking down at about one percent per second, the bleeding debuff flaring at him in sync with his frenzied heartbeat.

A cold nose bumped Tony's clenched fist and a notification flashed:

> Small Dog Wishes to join your Party!
> Do you accept?
> Yes   No

Tony accepted without a second thought and time dilated, slowing to a crawl as more windows populated his vision.

> Congratulations! You have successfully rescued your Spirit-Tied Pet! Would you like to name him now?

Tony accepted the prompt and a set of status bars appeared below his own.

> Maximus: Level 5 Dog (Warrior) Companion
> HP: 47   % MP: 100%   Stamina: 25%

Learn more in the companion Sub-Menu!

He had gotten there just in the nick of time.

Three things happened at once: the remaining five coyotes surged at the newly bonded pair, Tony readied himself, and the little dog barked. Tony swore he heard the word "sword" when it did.

I have a sword, Tony remembered, *I have TWO swords!*

Fighting a coordinated pack of coyotes in and of itself would be a difficult task for a solo combatant. Doing so unarmed was asking for a bad time.

He activated "Summon Dreadblade" and one of the wounded coyotes combusted in a shower of viscera and bone as a seven-foot-long great sword made of pitted steel tore out of its body and into Tony's grip. The Dread Knight carried the momentum through in a cleaving strike, slashing through two of the remaining beasts.

One of the coyotes latched onto Tony's forearm and the other nearly made it past him. Tony shoved his leg out to intercept the wild hound and its jaws closed around his ankle. They both thrashed wildly, tearing at his meager armor and HP with startling efficiency. Tony released his Dreadblade and slammed his fist into the beast on his arm.

Tony's HP dropped to ten percent, blurring his vision in a ruddy hue and a buff appeared under his status bars.

[Buff ID: InV4L1D] Query//Runtime 12s//Fetch//Error 504: Host Body Control Shift
WE ARE L3&10N YOU ARE 0NE: Damage Reduction increased by 15% per 10% HP missing. All Damage increased by 75% (Rage State)

We will not serve a weak king. One who hesitates to use his power. We will show you, a taut, grating voice echoed through the whole of Tony's being.

His body moved on its own, gripping the stunned monster by its snout and tearing it and the spine from the beast. It died instantly in the gruesome display of raw strength and malice.

Tony's chewed leg shot forward and skyward as if readying for an ax-kick. The coyote soared from the limb and Tony's right arm reached for his fallen blade. He felt his grip tighten like it had when he re-summoned the Essence Blade and the weapon started to float.

Hey! What do you think you're doing? Give me back my body! he challenged the voice.

Watching his body move without controlling it scared him almost as much as the prospect of losing Max. If whatever force possessing him was rounded on the dog next, he didn't know what he would be able to do to stop it. His right arm shot forward, sending the blade careening through the air and the coyote.

When next we return, you had better be ready, the voice menaced.

A burning sensation crawled through his veins until it reached his toes and fingertips as control returned. A tremendous weight fell onto his frame.

Tony's eyes rolled up to his status bar; the buff was gone with no debuff to replace it. He focused on his combat log and was greeted with a glitched screen, filled with fractured code and characters from the moment that he heard the voice. Tony shook his head, immediately regretting the action as his temples throbbed.

A quest notification popped into his vision.

You have completed the Familiar Quest: Man's Best Friend! Bonus! Your Spirit-Tied Pet took no additional damage from the encounter!

Item Received: Maximus's Tags – Soulbound Item In the event that your Spirit-Tied Pet falls in battle, use this item to summon him! Cooldown – 8 hours

Tears welled in Tony's eyes and he sank to his knees, immediately beset by puppy kisses. The concern over the mystery debuff, the strain on his body from thirty minutes of sprinting, and lingering pain from his wounds were gone. Licked away by his best friend.

He had done it. He had saved Maximus. He would never be without him again.

Chapter XI: Forlorn Flagship Reclamation

Tony took Maximus in his arms and strode out of the forest, the dog's curled tail thumping against Tony's ribs, his Dreadblade slung across his back and held in place by the Pauldron of Vengeance, right next to Jorogu's Marital Blade. He had a clear line of sight to the crashed ship, so he took the time to review his sheet and shore up the rest of his unspent points.

Character Sheet

Name: Antonious King   Race: Human (Ascendant)

Essence: 2 (Dormant)

Class: Squire (5) | Knight (5) | Dread Knight (2)

Attributes

Strength: 19+   Charisma: 10   Intelligence: 10

Dexterity: 14+   Wisdom: 11   Wits: 13+

Endurance: 18+   Spirit: 19+   Luck: 10

Skills

Melee – 10   Awareness – 5+   Occult – 5

Survival – 3+   Fortitude – 6+   Athletics – 4

Tandem Tactics: (5)

Sagas:

Active Saga: War Against Heaven

Backgrounds:

Artifact: Pauldron of Vengeance

Familiar: Maximus

Talents

Witness the Beginning

Summon Dreadblade (Life-Biting Essence)   Berserker's Stance

Pommel Strike   Oath   Charge   Invincible Will

New Fatal Resolve   *New* Adamant Slash

Tony had used his two remaining talent points to pick up Fatal Resolve and Adamant Slash and though he did not relish the idea of getting into another fight soon, he was excited to try them both.

Fatal Resolve: Channel your defiance to rebuke Death itself
Cost: 75 Lore   Duration: 2 minutes
Healing: 50% of Damage Received   Cooldown: 2 hours
Effect: Upon reaching critical HP the Dread Knight may activate this talent, taking no further Damage for two minutes. Once two minutes have passed, fifty percent of the damage received post-activation will be converted to HP.

Fatal Resolve was his first "second wind" talent, upping his survivability considerably. Tony's overall resilience had gone up drastically with the recent points added to his Attributes and Skills. Fortitude not only allowed him to resist debuffs like poison, fatigue, and disease, reduced the effective time of any debuffs he had, but it also gave him additional HP when he leveled. Tony doubted that he could have survived the blast that hit D, but he may be able to survive the first one that Ignacious shot at him.

Adamant Slash: Convert Lore to raw lethal force and vanquish those that oppose you

Cost: Variable   Cooldown: None
Range: 10 meters   Damage: Variable (Low to Immense)
Effect: Convert Lore to bonus damage to be inflicted at range. Each increment of 10 Lore spent will increase the bonus damage by 1 factor.
Note: Channeling Adamant Slash through any weapon not soulbound to the Dread Knight will destroy it.

Tony was glad to know beforehand that trying to use Adamant Slash with the Marital Blade would have disastrous consequences, both for the sword and for his recently formed relationship with Jorogu.

Satisfied with his selections and the way that his build was moving, Tony examined his new resource: Lore. Mana, or MP, like his HP and Stamina, would start as a full bar and empty as it was used. The Lore bar started empty and would fill as soon as combat started, according to the voice that read to him when he focused on his Lore Bar.

Lore: The Resource used by Dread Knights to fuel their talents. Lore builds with the pace of battle and is absorbed by the Dreadblade from fallen enemies. Using additional Lore when deploying talents could generate additional effects!

Lore reminded Tony of the Rage and Focus bars that older MMOs like WoW had used during the dark times of Microtransactions and "Pay-to-Win" scandals.

His Knight talents were now completely cooldown-based, having lost their Mana costs since he didn't have Mana anymore. In a fight, he would have to use his Talents carefully to build up enough Lore to activate his Dread Knight Talents.

Tony's and Auren's eyes met as he crested the furrow in the earth where the ruined craft rested. The God's eyebrows arched. "You leave for five minutes, and you not only return with a puppy but the Dread Knight Advanced Specialization?"

"Yup," Tony replied flatly, ignoring how off Auren's timekeeping was, "but hey, at least I didn't teleport someone across time and space under the guise that they were playing a video game."

Auren winced, then quirked his head. "Wait, what happened to the timid kid from the ship?" he asked half laughing. "You fight off a horde of spiders, get pseudo-engaged, and run off into the woods and you think that you can just come back here and talk to me like that?"

"Ignacious killed Demnas trying to kill me and coyotes tried to eat my dog," Tony started, some of the words catching in his throat. "D didn't need to die and I lost this little guy once already. I don't really care what level you are, God or not, you lied to me. You took me from my home and then couldn't be bothered to tell me the truth. The timid kid is taking a break."

And he's probably never coming back, Tony thought.

A smirk broke out across Auren's face. "Look, Ant-" he started before Tony's glare snapped back to bore into the God's eyes. "Tony, I get that you're upset-"

"Upset?" Tony challenged. "Upset is what I used to get when I got scheduled for overtime at work, upset is what I would get when I forgot to charge my bike's batteries and it broke down. If that's what upset is, how am I supposed to feel when I find out that I've been shanghaied out of my own reality and flung fifteen hundred years into the future?"

Auren raised his hands in surrender. "I can get us back to the Flagship, but I'll be vulnerable after we teleport, and we both know that there is a mole on the ship. Odds are, whoever that is will be waiting for us to come back."

You have been offered a quest!

Crimson Guard Duty: Protect Auren after arriving back on the Ascendant Flagship!

Rewards: XP | Dread Knight Set Piece | Ascendant Attribute Boost (Pending Ascension)

"Fine, let's do it," Tony agreed.

Auren stood with his back against Tony's and began to chant under his breath as lines of arcane fire burned into the ground.

Maximus whined softly as the air charged with magic. Tony ran his fingers through the coarse fur on the pup's neck and he soothed.

"It'll be okay, boy. We'll get you cleaned up and find some good food soon." The little dog nuzzled back into his arms as reality folded in around them.

A swirling hall of neon flame and sparks rushed by the two of them. There was no sound, no wind, and though Tony could tell that they weren't "moving" he could feel a pull from the middle of his chest toward a gleaming white point in the distance. He continued to pat Maximus, taking in his familiar, and unfortunately amplified, musk. In all of the strangeness of the new world he was a part of, Tony was glad for the one constant in Maximus to ground him.

As they drew nearer to the light at the end of the tunnel, Tony could feel the strain in Auren's back. In *Godmaker* Auren could be built as a combat caster or a brawler-mage hybrid class.

His talents had never allowed for teleportation between planets, let alone galaxies. It seemed that the Battle Aura was an incredibly variable resource for the God, and though he may only be limited by his imagination in its capabilities, using it for purposes that it was not intended for limited its use.

The steel halls of the Flagship started to fold in around them as they breached the gleaming point. Neither Tony nor Auren were prepared for what they saw.

Silence greeted them as they returned, broken bodies, blood, intestines, and shattered limbs covered the once-pristine floors and walls.

Time Remaining until Auren has recovered: 180 seconds

The hair on the back of Tony's neck and arms stood on end and Maximus let out a low growl. He knew better than to ignore instinct. The sound of metal flying through the air met Tony's ears as he spotted the glint of flying steel. He twisted, shielding Auren, and most importantly, Maximus, from the incoming javelin.

Your Luck has increased!

The tip of the javelin ricocheted off of the pitted metal of his Dreadblade. Tony tucked Maximus under Auren's half-collapsed and gasping frame and turned to face the attacker.

"So, you have made it back! Good, I was beginning to get bored!" Tolik's jovial voice boomed. "Murder is such a trivial business. I'm looking forward to a *real* fight! You won't disappoint me, will you, Antonious?"

Saga Effect Activated: Dire Battle
You are about to enter conflict with a member of The Cadre of Judgement. Death is Final.
Encounter XP increased by 25%!

Chapter XII: Grudge Match Rematch

Tolik strode out from the shadows of the battle-marred corridor. The wrecked Squire's Set he had worn in the Pits was replaced with a set of gleaming full plate, articulated and modified for maximum mobility and protection. The glowing yellow dot above his head, the sign of a Human Ascendant "player," was wreathed in streaks of black.

"Tolik? You're the Mole?" Tony asked.

"Mole? No. Do I look like a naked rodent, Antonious?" Tolik let the bladed haft of a wicked halberd sink into the metal floor, punctuating his indignation. "I am *the* assassin sent by the Holiest to destroy the Ascendant Program from the inside! The perfect crime, don't you think? An Ascendant to destroy the Ascendants!"

While Tony couldn't see Tolik's face through the slits of his helmet's visor, he could hear the smile in his voice.

He really thinks this is the right thing to do. Tony's blood turned to ice. *An Ascendant to destroy the Ascendants?*

"Why are you doing this, Tolik? Why work for Ignacious? After what he did to the Earth? What do you get out of it?" he demanded.

Tony could feel anger building in his chest, a demand for action, to do *something*. But he had to know and if he could buy a few seconds he could figure out just how he was going to beat Tolik a second time.

Name: Tolik Verräter   Level: 16   Race: Human (Ascendant)

Class: Squire   Specialization: Myrmidon   Essence: 4

"Why wouldn't I? Ascendants are immortal! Only Ignacious and the Cadre of Judgement have the means to keep us dead," the large man explained.

"So that's it? That's why? Because you don't want to be killed?" Tolik shrugged. Tony gulped. The ease of the gesture under at least fifty pounds of armor concerned him. Tony was still in starting gear, with the exception of his newly acquired weapons and the Pauldron of Vengeance.

"Do you wish to die? After knowing the power granted to us through Ascendance, this system, would you throw that away if you had the chance to preserve it?"

Tolik's rebuttal caught Tony in the chest like a fist. "I will make this offer to you once, Antonious. Step aside, that I may end that false god. Let me bring you before Ignacious, Holiest of the Divine, and I promise no harm will come to you." His armored fist released from his weapon and extended an armored hand.

> You have been offered a Quest!
> Abandoned Post: Betray the Ascendant Program
> Rewards: XP | Equipment | Safe Passage to Ignacious's
> Stronghold
> Note: Accepting this Quest will resolve the Saga: War Against
> Heaven without rewards

Tony stared at the quest window for what felt like a long time. Demnas had given his life for Tony for some reason he didn't understand, Auren had lied to him, and he didn't know if there would be another shot at immunity, let alone one that would let him keep his powers.

He looked down at his hands and then back toward Auren and Maximus. *Which answer is the right one?* Tony's eyes passed over the carnage left by Tolik's rampage. Unmoving faces, expressions frozen forever in death stared back at him. There were so many of them, so many killed. "Did they get the same offer?" Tony asked.

"Why does that matter? I am making this offer to you now. You have potential, Antonious, it would be a shame to waste it." The concern in Tolik's voice rang hollow.

He's scared, I beat him before and if I beat him again he fails, Tony rationalized. Tolik *shouldn't* be afraid of him, but he recognized the behavior.

Unseated champions frequently maintained an irrational fear of those that dethroned them; this could be manipulated or it could be a tremendous motivator. *I'm going to have to be careful.*

"I'm gonna have to pass," Tony said.

"That is a shame. You should consider yourself lucky, Antonious-"

"Stop calling me that," Tony menaced, temper surging back over his rational thought.

"I have been gifted the knowledge by our God Ignacious of how to grant final death. I will put you to rest, then the imposter, and I will be rewarded." With that, Tolik snapped his gauntleted fist around the haft of his poleaxe, held it tight to his side, and braced a tower shield against his body.

Tolik rushed him and an icon flashed underneath his status bars:

> Dire Battle – XP increased by 25% – Final Death will occur if defeated

Tony unslung Jorogu's Marital Blade and the Pauldron of Vengeance pulsed with blazing white energy.

Pauldron of Vengeance – +20% Damage Resistance, +10% Damage Dealt per 10% HP Missing, +2 Lore per second

Was that what happened in the woods?

Tony activated Knight's Charge in response. From a neutral standing position, he was parallel to the ground and halfway to the traitor.

Tolik faltered by half a step, not expecting an under-geared opponent to meet his advance so readily. The split-second of hesitation was exactly what Tony needed.

He dodged to Tolik's shield side and swept his blade up in a vertical slash against the surface of the tower shield, halting Tolik's momentum and rocking him back onto his heels. The muscles in Tony's back, shoulders, and arms strained under the force of the impact. Tony adjusted his grip, bringing his sword overhead to bring it crashing down onto the shield.

I might not be able to get past that thing, but if I can keep it busy and keep Tolik from making slashing attacks, I might be able to get him to drop it.

The spear tip of Tolik's halberd snuck out and glanced across Tony's side, leaving a deep red gash despite the crackling white energy that deflected the blow.

Tony's Lore bar shot up to three-quarters full as the pain burned through his ribs.

Fifteen percent of his HP bar emptied; even with the damage reduction offered by the matching set of Squire gear and the bonus from the Pauldron of Vengeance.

He wouldn't be able to take many more of those.

Tony reared back again in an exaggerated motion, baiting a counterattack or a shield slam. In the instant that Tolik moved from the guard, Tony willed the Marital Blade to affix itself to his shoulder and summoned the Dreadblade into his waiting hands, slashing down at the off-center shield with a roar.

As the blade collided with the steel wall Tony activated Adamant Slash. Activating the ranged Talent in immediate proximity was something he should have tested before trying it in combat where death was final. *Gotta pull out all the stops when you're the underdog,* he rationalized.

The Dreadblade thrummed violently in his grip and the blade glowed a deep violet before the blast discharged.

> Lore Feedback: -10% HP

Tony was sent sprawling and off-balance. His skin burned with pricks and needles as the Lore's natural flow was disrupted. Tolik slammed into the far wall, shards of tower shield embedded in his armor and the wall he wrenched himself from. Tony could see the maddened glee in the traitor's eyes and the rictus grin plastered on his face through the newly made holes in the helmet's visor.

For someone wearing fifty or more pounds in armor, Tolik was back on his feet and after Tony faster than he would have liked.

The large man attacked relentlessly, a flurry of a dozen rapid jabs with the spear tip of the weapon, some landing, others serving to put Tony on the defensive and keep him there.

Unable to gain purchase against the juggernaut, Tony realized he was about to run out of room to go backward. A pile of debris and broken bodies lay just a couple of paces behind him, jagged steel and splintered bones protruding in all directions.

Tolik was setting him up for a final charge, to impale him on the spear and then on the pile. With the nicks and cuts that he'd suffered already, the charge would likely take the last of his health pool, and the rest would be overkill.

Mind racing in the moment before Tolik's attack, Tony found an answer. *Why that's crazy, Tony! So crazy, it just...might...work...* he mimicked the line from a terrible classic *The Master of Disguise* to himself.

Tolik leveled the tip of the weapon at him and surged forward. "This is where you die, little King!" Spittle flew from beneath the remnants of the helm's visor.

Tony sidestepped the charge to Tolik's inside, slamming against the man's bulk and armor, hitting twenty percent HP and activated Fatal Resolve.

He slammed into the pile of sharp objects. Blood, bone dust, and the contents of Tony's stomach covered the front of Tolik's armor. The large man relaxed as Tony's body slumped onto the pile. His task completed, the traitor turned to face Auren.

Maximus tried furiously to wriggle out of Auren's grip, whining and snarling. The nearly recuperated God held the pup tightly.

"And now, I kill the false deity. Are you ready to die, 'Lord' of Auras?" Tolik sneered. His gait was a confident swagger, like a linebacker who had just sacked a quarterback and wanted to gloat between plays.

"Look, Tolik," Auren started, getting up to his feet.

"Begging won't save you!" the large man shouted. Something caught in the corner of Auren's vision and he couldn't help but smirk.

"No, I literally mean look, behind you. You're not done yet." He pointed over Tolik's shoulder. Maximus stopped struggling and barked.

Tolik turned violently, his helmet finally succumbing to the wear of combat, flying off and clattering to the ground. "No, this is not possible! How are you-"

Tony's feet slammed to the metal floors, the echoes of the impact soon drowned out by the erratic electric snapping of the violet aura shrouding the Dread Knight. Jagged steel and splinters of bone protruded from his flesh.

He was one *angry* pin-cushion.

"Fuck you, that's how," he answered. Tony held his hand out for his Dreadblade and it obeyed, soaring from the floor into his waiting grip. "You can't kill me, Tolik, you never could. Seeing you fight in the arena was all I needed to figure you out." Tony's eyes flicked to his HP, which was still draining.

Bleeding: You have been impaled or cut badly. -1% HP per second x 5 [30 seconds Remaining]

Pauldron of Vengeance: Divine Damage Resistance has Activated Divine Damage Resistance: Damage-over-time durations are doubled and damage effects are halved

"No! That's not true! I have been gifted by the divine! Die!" Tolik swung the meaty ax-head at Tony. He didn't bother to dodge as the blade bit deep into his left shoulder.

The light that rose in Tolik's eyes was soon replaced with terror as Tony reached up and removed the blade from his body, letting the blade slam to the ground under Tolik's bulk just past his shoulder.

Status effects continuing to damage him through Fatal Resolve was not something Tony had accounted for. Even with the reduction of damage, the extended duration would still kill him if he didn't end this fight.

I'll keep pressing the intimidation factor, see if he won't surrender, he thought.

"I told you, Tolik. You. Can't. Kill. Me. Surrender now, while I'm feeling generous." Tony slammed his Dreadblade across Tolik's chest and activated Adamant Slash again. The large man slid back, blood seeping from the forming cracks in his armor; another Adamant Slash shattered the cuirass and put him flat on his back. "Now get up," Tony growled.

"No, please, mercy!" Tolik begged.

Tony bent down and grabbed Tolik by the scraps of metal left on his chest and hauled him to his feet. He opened his mouth to list the conditions of the large man's surrender and Tolik pulled a dagger from behind his back and drove it into Tony's chest. His Dreadblade clattered to the marred flooring.

Tony looked at the dagger, briefly to his debuffs, and then back to Tolik.

"Really? And here I was about to accept your surrender." Tony pivoted and threw Tolik into the wall, then ripped the dagger from his chest and threw it into the man's gut.

Tolik yelped in pain and surprise. "Mercy!"

"How many people here begged for mercy?" Tony screamed, his violet aura snapping with discharge. Bone shards and steel ejected violently from his skin, slamming into the steel floors and walls. Tony's blood splattered onto the floor. "How many?"

Tolik had no answer.

Tony held his right hand out for the Dreadblade and caught it halfway up the pitted edge, advancing on the defenseless traitor.

Tolik held his hands up in surrender, mumbling incomprehensible pleas. The Dread Knight closed the gap between them and grabbed the hilt of the dagger in his left hand, twisting it in the Myrmidon's guts.

Tolik screamed.

Tony slammed his Dreadblade into the traitor's open mouth and straight through to the metal wall. Tolik's eyes went wide before rolling back into his head. As his body started to slump, it dissolved into gold, white, and black motes of light.

> Quest Completed!
> Crimson Guard Duty: Protect Auren while he is vulnerable

The system told him as a rush of scarlet flame washed over Tony's body, forcing the wounds in his torso closed.

He watched the Bleeding Debuffs fall off and with the end of Fatal Resolve, his HP rested just over half full. Tony rolled his shoulders and cracked his neck before turning back to look at Auren. "So, now what?" he asked.

Auren looked back at him, eyes hard, and mouth a thin line. Maximus was still in his arms. Auren had one hand over the pup's eyes. "You killed him."

"Yes? What else was I supposed to do?" Tony answered.

"No, he was Ascended. Traitor or not, I should be getting a notice that an Ascendant has died and is in the queue for respawning. He's not."

"Did you get any of those notifications when he butchered everyone on board?" Tony was annoyed. A lot of this could have gone differently if Auren had just been honest with him.

"I only got notifications for Ascendants off-world in a queue to respawn here. You didn't activate any talents when you dealt the final blow, did you?"

Tony's brow furrowed. "I didn't do anything to him that I-"

Just then, a notification flashed in his vision.

Congratulations! Your Dreadblade has consumed an Ascended Soul!

Your Dreadblade has reached Level 5!

Customization options are now available!

Chapter XIII: Coming to Grips

Tony blinked in disbelief, staring wide-eyed at the notification. "I think my sword ate him."

"Your think your sword WHAT?" Auren shouted. "How?"

"Well, I just got a notification that my Dreadblade consumed an Ascended Soul and leveled up a bunch. I didn't-"

> Awards Amended!
> Quests Completed: Crimson Guard Duty
> Sidequest: Whack-a-mole Completed! Check your Quest Log for rewards!

"Never mind, there it is, notifications about quest rewards."

"Closing in on Ichor-Seeking Blade are we? Any specific intentions with that talent?" Auren's tone sent a chill down Tony's spine; his voice was cold and detached.

"Yeah, introduce my sword to Ignacious's face, a lot." Tony tensed. He didn't like where the line of questioning was headed. He'd made the decision on the fly and it seemed like the best option.

"Check your rewards, we'll talk about this after you sort yourself," Auren ordered, turning his back on Tony and crossing his arms.

"What do you mean 'sort myself?' You're the one that's got me out here on a one-man crusade against the Cadre of Judgement!" Auren scowled at him from over his shoulder. "Of course I'm going to bee-line for Ichor-Seeking Blade, I'm going to need *every* advantage I can get to stand a *chance,* let alone win."

Auren whipped around and advanced, jabbing his finger into Tony's chest. "And what happens after? What if you win? You kill Ignacious, suck him up in that doom weapon, then what? You'll just ride off into the cosmos, never to be feared by mortal or god?"
Tony hesitated for a moment. He hadn't thought that far ahead, what would he do? What would be expected of him?

"Why would anyone fear *me* after all this? Ignacious is the one out there terrorizing the known universe, *if* we win, all of that stops. How do I become the bad guy after that?" Tony slapped Auren's hand away and shoved him. To his surprise, Auren staggered back a couple of steps.

Auren glared at him, scoffed, and stormed off.
Your Social Link with Auren has suffered

Yeah, no shit, Tony thought at the system as he willed his menus to open, focusing on his Quest Log.
Quest Rewards:
Crimson Guard Duty: 1200 XP
Select a Dread Knight Gear Piece!

Witness the Beginning
Gauntlets   Helm   Cuirass

Tony focused on the Helmet option. He had nothing in his helmet slot and an improvement there would go miles. He was presented with two options:

Visage of the Forsaken: A faceless armored mask, once worn by a fearless swordsman
Rarity: Unique   Quality: Exceptional
Defense Rating: +5   Slot: Helmet
Effects: +15% Bonus to Stealth and Disguise
Activated Abilities: 赤い川を走る "Run the Red River"

As appealing as a bonus to anonymity was, given his chat with Auren, stealth was way out of his wheelhouse.

The Doomed King's Helm: Armor of a king who led his men into battle, knowing he led them all to their deaths
Rarity: Unique   Quality: Exceptional
Defense Rating: +10   Slot: Helmet
Effects: +5% Defense Rating vs Projectiles
Activated Abilities: MOΛΩN ΛABE "Come and Take Them"

Tony elected for the latter and a spartan-esque helmet appeared in his inventory. He hadn't interacted with the Inventory system before now, as most of what he had, he was wearing.

The base inventory was limited to sixteen slots. The items inside were manipulated by will alone, meaning that if he had health potions or other consumables inside, he only had to think about using them to do so.

Tony willed the helmet out of his inventory and it dropped into his hands, prompting a system message to appear in the center of his vision:

Equip Helmets outside of Combat?

Yes   No

(Any effects or boosts will be in effect outside of combat)

Tony selected the "No" option, the helm equipped in the formerly empty helm slot. He felt stronger, sharper, more aware, and decided that he would go over his character sheet with a fine-toothed comb later.

The Pauldron had activated at the start of combat and made up for some of the gaps between Tony and Tolik. The disturbing thing was that the Pauldron had activated on its own. Upon examining the Pauldron of Vengeance, he noticed that there was no trigger, no command word, just plus twenty defense rating and level counters.

Level counters? What are those for?

Tony cruised through his character sheet; there was still so much he didn't know about the game.

What was Essence? What do Sagas do besides try to kill him? There hadn't been time to sit and figure it all out since he arrived "in-game." Everything had happened so fast; it was a lot to take in.

Not actually being in a game, but having all of the same functions of one, having scores of powerful beings out for his head, the other two hundred allies that he was supposed to have had been killed by Tolik, allegedly, and D had sacrificed himself so Tony could live.

For what?

Tony could feel a tightness well up in his chest, a swelling that was a tell-tale sign of a full-blown anxiety attack waiting to rock his world. Rationally, Tony knew he needed to take the time to break this down, process it, and accept it, but he didn't. He put it in a box and stashed it for later.

As much as Tony was furious with him, Auren was his only source of information, and besides Maximus, the only one on his side. Even if the God couldn't, he needed to be the bigger person and make things right between them.

The Lord of Auras was not hard to find. Tony closed his menus, and a few paces away, Auren's footprints had started to scorch the steel flooring. A couple of halls and turns later, Tony found him in a control room, reviewing the damages to the Flagship's systems.

Judging by the sour look on his face, he was either still *really pissed* at Tony, or the damage was severe.

Not one for subtlety or great skill in starting the conversation, Tony led with a question that had bothered him for a while now, "Auren, what was D the god of?"

"Hmm?" Auren looked up at Tony from the terminal, his mind coming back to the moment.

"Demnas was the God of Ascendants."

"Wait, what? I thought the Ascendant Program was a new thing?" Tony couldn't tell if he was more confused or concerned by the revelation.

"New in implementation, not in concept. D was the first that we pulled through and into a compatible body. Thinking back that far, it was kind of strange. He took to the Program so fast." A note of nostalgia rang through Auren's voice.

"Were the two of you close?" Tony asked.

"Very," Auren started. "A decade after his Ascendance, Demnas went even higher, deifying. We didn't even think that was possible, but once we thought about it, an Ascendant becoming a god wasn't that strange. Demnas *believed* in the Program, not just beating Ignacious, but restoring freedom to the cosmos."

"We?"

"Yes, Morkhan and I," Auren answered.

"Morkhan, the Sage?"

Auren chuckled. "Morkhan has not been addressed as 'Sage' in more than two thousand years, but yes the very same."

Godmaker had been his go-to game, the first game he had ever gone full try-hard completionist on.

Tony could feel the wheels turning in his head. There was more to the current situation, something that he wasn't seeing.

"Auren, how 'true' are the events that happened in 'Godmaker?' Like, is that the recollection of the war against the Titans or something more?"

"They should be pretty spot on. We used the game system's onboard tech to turn play hours into 'worship' to leverage against the Titans and preserve the cosmos. While, yes, it was a 'retelling' of the war, the prison that the Titans are locked away in requires a lot of Essence to keep them there." Tony paced and nodded along with Auren's explanation.

"Did you know about the secret endings?" he asked, not looking up from his point of focus.

"There were four I think-" Auren looked up and away, counting on his fingers.

"There were five," Tony corrected.

"Five?"

"Yeah, if you had Ignacious in your party for the final battle, and had his Guile higher than his Strength stat and a maxed-out Combat Trick Tree, there was a secret ending where Morkhan gave him the Mantle of the Gods. The net went crazy after it was discovered, and if what you're saying about the worship-tech or whatever kept working after the battle against the Titans, that would explain why Ignacious has so much power for being such a shit-head. In all of the other endings, *you* were the one given the mantle, not him," Tony rattled off.

Godmaker had gotten a random content patch more than three years after the release of its final DLC; no one could figure out what it added. Hackers that tried to access the game files in the content patch on the server-side ended up with wiped saves and the members of the *Godmaker* community who dropped leaks when new content released had known nothing about it.

Auren shook his head. "I wouldn't be surprised that Ignacious would pull something like that, he is a vain asshole, but Morkhan was the one who stalled Ignacious so we could get the Ascendant program off the ground."

"Who else has access to Ignacious and the Program?"

"I don't like where your head's at, Tony," Auren warned.

Tony ignored it. "Even with Tolik here as a mole, I have a hard time believing that if your fighters have long-distance cloaking that the Flagship doesn't, or at least a way to stop transmissions from leaving the ship from unknown frequencies? It would make sense that Morkhan's clairvoyance would let him keep tabs on you and report back to Ignacious-"

"Enough!" Auren shouted, Battle Aura flaring. "I will tolerate much from you, Antonious, but I. WILL. NOT. TOLERATE-"

Maximus barked, utterly halting the momentum of Auren's fury.

Soul Download Complete. Respawn Commencing. Warning: Spawn Table has been damaged. Please socket Genesis Pod to start Respawn

The message blinked on the terminal screen and repeated.

Soul Download Complete. Respawn Commencing. Warning: Spawn Table has been damaged. Please socket Genesis Pod to start Respawn

WARNING: Respawn Systems Critical. Current Queue will be lost without repair.
Current Ascendant Souls in Queue: 227 Progress of Current Spawn: 17%

You have been offered a Quest!
Shepherd of Lost Souls: Find a way to get the Spawning Tables back online
Rewards: XP | Unseen Ally Background | Ascendant Military Force

Tony accepted the quest that popped up in his vision without reading the description. "Shepherd of Lost Souls" gave him all the context he needed. The quest arrow popping into his vision after accepting was all that he needed to take off at a full sprint.

That son of a bitch was bluffing, Tony thought. Tolik had managed to kill the other Ascendants on the ship, but he hadn't been able to *kill* them. Tony looked down to the sound of soft pads and claws tapping on metal; Maximus was keeping up with him easily. He couldn't help but smile.

The small dog met Tony's gaze for a moment, looking at him with all of the unconditional love that only a dog can have for one person.

We're gonna be just fine.

Chapter XIV: A Matter of Willpower

Tony followed the quest arrow pointing him toward the Respawn Chamber, Maximus barely a pace behind him. Every few paces he would hear the blaring announcement from the ship's AI about the respawn failing. Tony pumped his legs, willing himself to reach maximum speed.

Shortcut Available. Would you like to start Freerunning?

Yes   No

With your current Athletics Skill Rank, Freerunning will decrease your travel time by 6.2%

Tony focused on the "Yes" option and the quest arrow melded to the floor, showing him a path to traverse. Tony reached down to his belt and drew the dagger he had taken from Tolik during their fight.

6.2%? he thought. *Let's see if we can make that 10.*

A sharp right into a maintenance corridor was the first diversion from his previous path. Tony slid, the hard soles of his boots skittering over the rivets in the floor paneling. What he was about to try would either work out in his favor or tear his arm out of its socket.

Tony plunged the first inch and a half of the dagger into the floor and used the sharp change in momentum to sling himself into the maintenance corridor and maintain his speed. He almost lost his hold on the dagger in the "swing" but it came free at the last second.

Low pipes, hanging conduits, and wires cluttered the hall. The navigation showed a winding path around the major obstructions; Tony had never been the best at following directions. Sliding the dagger back into his belt as he moved, he vaulted off of the wide pipe in front of him, grabbed a fistful of coated wires, and went horizontal "running" along the wall for a few paces, then used a rigid conduit as a makeshift trapeze to clear an elevated vent and reorient his feet with the floor.

Nav showed a sharp left coming as he neared the end of the maintenance hall. Tony retrieved the dagger and flipped it over to his left hand, stabbing it into the corner of the wall as he slid around the corner.

A snap and a stumble through a bunch of crates later, Tony looked down at the blade of the dagger. He'd lost the point as well as the top third of the blade. Tony grimaced and discarded the broken weapon. He hopped through a few broken windows and vents and slid to a stop in front of the Respawn Chamber.

Travel time reduced by 7.2%

Tony shook his head as he jogged into the room. It was a massive enclosure with pods filled with an azure glowing liquid, tables lined with circuitry, and myriad displays along the walls. Lines upon lines of data scrolled angrily across a majority of them, far too much info for Tony to process. Auren and Maximus arrived just a second later, snapping him out of a stupefied stare. His eyes caught a flash of light on the far side of the room and he jogged over.

A body was being constructed on the table. Well, trying to be constructed. The network of blood vessels, nerves, bones, and magical conduits were forming as expected, but at the generation of muscle tissue, the process would fail.

Whoever this was, if they weren't able to correct the respawn error, they'd be subjected to an infinite "loading screen" until the system completely failed and they died, for good.

Tony observed the process twice before he stepped in. When the process reset, all that remained was a locus of light over the center of where the body had been. The spawning table itself was more like the bed to a 3D printer and an orb above the table was the printing nozzle.

The covered wires that connected to the "nozzle" were trashed; someone had tried to cut the cords housed within the tubes and had almost succeeded.

There were six spawning tables in this room and eight pods. If he had to guess, the tables handled the direct respawning and the pods handled regeneration.

Tony stared up at the mangled wires and cords. Some of them were hovering just a few inches from each other, some still intact even.

"Hm, I think that if that wire can be bridged then the process will finish," Tony thought aloud.

"And how do you suggest we do that?" Auren answered.

"I don't know, you're the god here." He hadn't seen how any of the machinery in the flagship functioned or what actually powered it. Essence fueled almost everything in Godmaker; there was no reason to assume differently here. He decided to query the system.

> Command//: Roll Intelligence + Occult – Query: How to complete the Essence circuit.

To Tony's delight, the system chirped back at him.

Rolling Intelligence Attribute and Occult Skill. . . Success!
An Essence Circuit can only be completed by living matter or material designed to transfer Essence at high rates.

Tony groaned, squatted to pat Maximus on the head, and said, "Don't pull me off until the lights shut out, or you'll get zapped too."

"I wouldn't really-" Auren started.

"I was talking to the dog," Tony cut him off with a smirk. Auren crossed his arms and smirked back.

Tony jumped up and caught the higher end of the cable and a buff appeared under his status bars.

> Charged – Your Lore generation is increased by 150%

He swung and reached down with his other hand and snatched the end of the dangling cable. As soon as his grip closed around it his hands locked and every muscle in his body flexed and went taut at once. A debuff accompanied the "Charged" buff.

> Overcharged – 10% HP loss per second

He smelled his flesh burning, felt his nerves frying, and heard his heart pounding in his ears. He would only have to hold the wires together for a few more seconds. Leaning down, he saw skin forming over the muscles, followed swiftly by clothing. He let go of the top wire and was shot clear across the room by a violent discharge of essence.

"Respawn Complete," the Flagship's female AI voice stated. Tony groaned as he got to his feet, his HP at thirty percent.

The body on the table belonged to an Ashtar woman clad in furs. Teeth and claws made up the fastenings of her armor and her head was half shaved, her hair was crystalline and translucent, smooth to the point where it was tied, and from there it was dreadlocked adorned with sigiled beads.

Her grey eyes snapped open and locked with Tony's, flashing blue. He felt like she could see out through the back of his skull.

"Good mor-" She flicked her wrist at him and at least a cup of water splashed over his face and into his mouth. He wiped his face.

"What are you-" She splashed him again. Tony spit out a mouthful of water, careful not to spit on her and opened his mouth to speak, but was met with more water for his efforts.

Tony put one hand on his hip and the other in front of his face. "Could you stop that? I'm trying to talk to you!"

"Why won't that debuff go away?" Her voice sounded familiar, but Tony couldn't place it. Tony looked at his status bars and was surprised to see his HP back to sixty percent.

Marred Destiny – Your fate is in flux and uncertain [Source: Active Saga]

"It's from a Saga that I have active, I don't think those can be cleansed," he answered truthfully. Some people in full immersion MMOs, which Ascendant Online was specifically not, could be jerks, and plan counter builds around someone they planned to troll. It was entirely possible that they were the only two Ascendants left in the "program" and unless the flagship got some major repairs, no one else would be respawning any time soon.

"Oh, well, that's irritating," she said. Then she looked around. "What did you do?" she half yelled.

"I literally just got here, not even twenty minutes ago. I didn't do this."

"Then what the hell happened?"

"Auren, D, and I left to grind on Arach. We came back here and Tolik had pretty much killed everyone on board, so I killed him back."

"Tolik? Really? What an ass." She sat up and looked at Tony like a lynx sizing up a squirrel. "And you killed him? All on your own? What level are you?" She was asking a lot of questions.

"Yes, yes, and level twelve." She arched an eyebrow at that.

"Level twelve, not bad. Tolik was level fifteen when I saw him before I left. You must either have some crazy equipment, which you don't," she said astutely, "or have been either really lucky or really smart with how you beat him."

"Little bit of B and C," Tony answered.

He jumped at the feeling of a cold nose pressing into his hand. "Hey boy," he said, reflexively scratching the pup behind the ears.

The woman glared at him, shot to her feet, and stormed out of the room. Tony glanced at Auren, then the door, and back. The God shrugged at Tony.

"I think I'm going to let her cool off a little. Are the teleporters still active?"

"That's probably a good idea, Vasna tends to swing first and ask questions later. You were lucky," Auren got the faraway look he did whenever he was reviewing notifications or otherwise looking into the system. "They should be. Where are you going?"

"I think I'm going to head back to Arach. See if there's some more grinding I can do there and meet the Spider Queen."

"Are you sure that's a good idea?" Auren asked.

"What's the worst that could happen?" Tony retorted.

Chapter XV: Erudition of Tradition

Tony walked into the personnel warp chambers, a smattering of pads and panels were spread across the muddled space. Splotches of dried blood told a story of failed escape attempts during Tolik's onslaught. Tony pushed the imagery building in his head down. Those people had been avenged through Tony's action, for better or worse.

They're all in the respawn queue, there's nothing else I can do about that right now, he justified. He needed to get away from the damn ship. Everywhere he looked there was death and while Arach was where this whole mess really got out of hand, it was where he found Maximus and Jorogu.

That was another thing he had to figure out, the sword Jorogu gave him.

Jorogu's Marital Blade	Rarity: Unique (1 of 1)
Durability: 100%	Enchantments: Concealed (Social Link 5)
Slashing Damage: Exceptional	Thrusting Damage: Good
Parry: Good	Riposte Multiplier: 3.75x

The item name suggested that it was a kind of marriage contract. Tony thought back on what Jorogu said when she gave him the blade.

"Since I separated these legs from my body and lost the duel, I cannot re-assimilate them. It is only right that you should take it with you."

"It is only right..." Tony repeated. Did besting Jorogu in the duel mean she had been obligated to propose? He scratched the back of his head as he stepped onto one of the warp pads.

"Please enter Warp Coordinates," the ship's AI chirped through the panel. Tony swiped his hand at the screen and it followed the motion, gliding into arm's reach. He tapped "Arach" into the destination screen and it flashed an annoyed red at him.

"You must enter a more specific location," the AI scolded.

Tony rolled his eyes and tried tapping in 'Ascendant Crash Site,' another irritated flash.

Frustration welled up in his chest and for an instant, Tony considered putting his fist through the panel.

I just want to get out of here!

He took some deep steadying breaths. Breaking the panel wouldn't get him off the ship. Tony studied the screen, there were fields to enter traditional coordinates, keyword searches, dropdowns for systems, planets, hemispheres, and quadrants, but they had to be selected sequentially and he didn't know which system Arach was in. He swiped through the pages and nearly shouted with glee.

Sigil Entry

Tony rolled his arm over to get a good look at the mark Jorogu had given him, the sword with four sharpened prongs, and drew it in the Sigil window.

Sigil Accepted

Destination: Arach Empire Capital

WARNING

Warp Pads at Destination are not configured for return transport. Haght'anak access Key Required.

Tony paused. A one-way trip was *not* what he had in mind. He scrolled through the remaining pages to see if there was an access key listed, he even searched for it in the system. No dice. An idea sprang to mind as he stepped off the pad and approached one of those that were severely damaged.

Maybe the access key is a physical component?

He flipped over one of the panels and planted his rear on the floor to study it. Tony turned the damaged tech over in his hands, examining its exterior.

He'd scrapped cars for a short time to make money before landing his third shift work assignment and housing. Tony was in no way a mechanical genius, but, if he could take something apart he could usually figure out how it worked.

A thin but sturdy metal casing kept the interior from view, the glass screen was severely cracked, and none of the buttons responded to his prodding.

He didn't think that Auren or Vasna would be able to repair the damaged panel, let alone be in a civil enough mood for him to ask.

This was a panel he could break.

He grabbed a scrap of metal from the floor next to him and used it to pry the glass off, gaining only a couple of small cuts on his fingers for his efforts.

The guts of the panel reminded Tony of the inside of a PC more than he expected. Common components like RAM sticks, a CPU, Power source, and even a Hard Drive were easily identified. The parts he didn't recognize, Tony used the system to identify.

Essence Alternator: A piece of technology that converts battery charge to Essence

Guest Filter: A piece of technology that allows the owner of the Warp Pad to scan and either accept or reject incoming guests

Access Key Reader: A chip that resonates with a Pad Access Key to gain additional Warp Locations

Jackpot.

Tony tossed the remnants of the panel aside and got to his feet; he'd need to get into the guts of a pad to find an access key. He nudged the defunct pad with his foot. Without a panel, it wouldn't function so there was no harm in eviscerating the thing.

He squatted low and wrapped his fingers around the bottom of the pad; flexing the muscles in his legs and glutes, he stood and flipped the thing with a grunt.

Fortunately, the bottom was open, providing immediate access to the components. Not wanting to waste time, he used the system to find the Pad Access Key. It looked more like a spike with a dim green glow to it than a mechanical piece. He pried the few connecting wires from the key and pulled it free from the pad. "That should do it," he muttered.

Tony ventured back to the pad waiting for him to confirm the warp. Maximus sat there waiting, his curled tail thumping softly against the metal. Tony hoped that the Pad Access Key would allow him to return freely, otherwise, he'd have to use the Respawn option he'd seen in the menus and wait in the queue.

He pocketed the spike and confirmed the warp. The odd sensation of movement while standing still settled in, this time vertically, unlike when Auren had teleported them.

The light swirled from purple to blue, then red and the familiar orange starscape of Arach's system. His feet slammed into the blue-green grass, delightfully free of spilled spider ichor.

Maximus staggered around, clearly less accustomed to interdimensional travel than Tony was.

He scooped the small dog up in his arms and cradled him. A cold, wet nose pressing into his armpit made him jump and then smile.

Tony looked up to see two spider guards approaching him. They were in the same evolutionary state as Ama, the medic from the duel: spider bodies with humanoid torsos covered in shining chitin sprouting from the cephalothorax where the mandibles would be.

The pair leveled sword spears at him, Naginata if he remembered correctly. Their mouths opened and a series of clicks and hisses came out. He couldn't tell what they were saying, but it didn't sound like they were happy to see him. Maximus's head popped out of Tony's armpit with a snarling growl and bared teeth.

Little guy's got some fight in him! Tony thought.

"I am here to see Princess Jorogu. I mean no harm," he spoke slowly, hoping that the soldiers would understand him. They hesitated for a moment before one of them twisted their abdomen, spinnerets pointed directly at Tony. He sank into a ready stance on reflex and shielded Maximus's snarling face. He wasn't here to fight, but he'd be damned if anyone was going to go after his dog.

There was an eerie moment of stillness before a small spider, about the size of a chipmunk, skittered up onto the guard *not* pointing their web end at Tony.

The guard craned its neck as if listening to a secret being whispered into its ear. It nodded once, twice, and a third time, then held three fingers up at Tony and clicked at the other guard, who relaxed.

Tony gave it a two count before relaxing himself and scratched Maximus behind the ear, calming the savage beast. The guards waved him forward, indicating that he was to follow them.

He walked forward and the two guards circled him, looking him over thoroughly before he held up his arm with the mark. They stopped immediately, embarrassed surprise overwhelmed their facial expressions and they beckoned him urgently forward again.

Tony followed.

Chapter XVI: Bellicostic Béguin

Beyond the pair of guards were four more and what had to be the biggest tree Tony had ever seen, in-game or otherwise. It was like one of the capital multiplexes with skyscrapers for branches and yachts for leaves; dense webbing shrouded a majority of the tree and formed skyways between the larger areas. As he walked, flanked by the initial pair of guards, the others fell in around him.

Normally, being surrounded would have made Tony nervous, but the way the guards eyed other passing spiders gave him more of a "get down, Mr. President" vibe than anything.

Tony's head was on a swivel; the spiders of the cluster were in various stages of evolution. He guessed that they started off as eggs, then the chipmunk-sized spider he saw, giant spider, "rally" spider, the "Arachne" like the guards around him, and he assumed, the stage that Jorogu was in was their final evolutionary state.

He walked into the rear of the guard in front of him; they had stopped while he was distracted.

"Sorry! I'm sorry, about that whole, space thing. You probably can't understand a word I'm saying can you?" Tony rambled.

The guard turned back to glare at him and pointed up into the tree. He followed the gesture and looked back at the guard. The profound level of confusion that washed across his face was such that it transcended the language barrier between the two of them.

The guard smacked the previously pointing palm into its forehead, then with its foremost spider-legs, it pantomimed a climbing motion, one leg over the other and dragging down. Tony nodded, then looked down at Maximus. He was pretty certain he could make the climb, but not while carrying Max in his arms. The small dog looked up at him, eyes full of love, tail slapping against his side. "Don't worry, buddy, I'm not leaving you behind," he cooed. Tony looked around, trying to find an example of what he needed.

He spotted an Arachne with some webbing on her abdomen, spiderlings crawling in and out of the protective satchel. Tony cradled Max in one hand and used the free one to point at the dog, then to his back, and to the Arachne with the spiderlings. The guard gestured for him to repeat his "request" and he did so two more times. The guard nodded slowly and tapped two of the others with the haft of his spear. They exchanged a series of clicks and then set to spinning a sling pack out of webbing.

The first guard handed it to Tony and smiled at him, a rictus expression that showed row upon row of gleaming fangs. He reciprocated the expression and took the pack, slid Maximus inside, and then slung it over his shoulder. Tony shuffled around a little, trying to jostle the pup out of the makeshift sling. The pack was secure; Max's ears flopped around wildly with Tony's bounces, but he stayed right in place.

Tony nodded to the guard and then pointed up to the same point the guard had. The Arachne reciprocated the gesture and moved forward, spider legs working in tandem to propel it vertically into the tree. With a running start, Tony followed; reaching, grabbing, and pulling on instinct, he was surprised with the speed he was able to climb.

So were the guards, just not the same way. A few things became immediately apparent: the guards had been tasked with escorting Tony as soon as they saw his mark, the climb was going to be much more difficult than Tony had assumed, and the guards were getting bored by his comparatively sluggish pace. After ten minutes of scowls and exaggerated sighing clicks, Tony focused on his skills, specifically Athletics.

Skill Specialties: You may assign a specialty to any Skill with 3 or more Ranks

Skill Specialties grant additional competency when performing actions that are associated with the Sill Specialty

The available Specialties for Athletics were Distance Running, Feats of Strength, Aerobics, Sports, Tricky Maneuvers, Climbing, and Freerunning.

The choice was obvious, as useful as the Feats of Strength or Distance Running could be, he'd used Freerunning before to reduce travel time and it was immediately useful; he didn't want to be climbing all day. Confirming the specialization made the freerunning overlay appear in his vision, though much more subdued than when he had activated it on the ship.

Tony tightened his core and bunched his legs, launching himself at a highlighted branch then bunched his core muscles up and tucked his legs, uncorking as soon as he was upside-down and hurtling skyward. He grabbed another branch before he passed by and swung around, planting his feet on it in his best "Spider-Man" pose.

The Arachne guards clicked amusedly at each other and scuttled ahead of him in the branches, each holding out the hafts of their spears.

The guard closest to him wiggled the weapon with a "come on, this will be fun" expression on its face. His freerunning overlay shifted, showing him a path that used the guard's assistance and a predicted pattern that the guards would use with their current formation. Maximus started barking excitedly and pawing at Tony's shoulder.

I guess that answers that, Tony thought just before he looked over his shoulder to check on the small dog. He reached over and scratched behind the pup's ear. Tony looked up at the guard, making eye contact with its primary set of eyes, and nodded.

Tony launched himself at the guard and grabbed a hold of the spear. Before he could shift his momentum around the haft, the guard heaved and slung him toward the next guard in formation. Tony's breath caught in his chest with the sudden velocity and barely managed to wrap both hands around the polearm. He circled it once before being shot on to the next guard. The way they were moving him from one guard to the next reminded Tony of a nunchaku drill his instructors taught him early on in his training.

Making small circles after a sharp nunchaku strike allows you to maintain control of the weapon, to keep your chi in harmony. When you stop considering the weapon as part of your chi, you lose control, when you lose control, you surrender it to the enemy, when the enemy has control, you lose.

Hearing his instructor's words sharpened his focus. Though in this case, he was the "nunchaku," maintaining control over himself and using the overlay to know where he would travel next would allow him to complete his rapid trek without incident.

Tony, Maximus, and his escort of Arachne guards reached the midpoint of the entire structure in short order. The platform that he landed on spread on for miles. Branches and clusters of webbing sprouted up without rhyme or reason, and Arachne bustling between them. After watching for a couple of minutes, it clicked.

This is a marketplace! Tony realized. Eggs, bound in spider silk, seemed to be the currency but it looked to Tony that the size of the egg mattered more than the quantity.

"Antonious!" a voice called out. He whirled to see Jorogu, Ama, and a group of smaller but more "advanced" Arachne emerge from a particularly impressive bundle of web and branches.

Her spider legs retracted as she ran toward Tony and nearly slammed into him as she wrapped her arms around his waist. Tony's eyebrows reached his hairline when she planted her lips firmly against his, old habits kicked in and Tony sank into the embrace and matched it. Maximus's ill-timed "woof" caused Jorogu to giggle and pull back.

"Who's this? Did you bring me a snack?" she asked.

"Huh? Oh! No, this is Maximus, he's my familiar, and is uh, not for snacking," he said.

"Oh, well that's alright then. Maximus is a cute one, takes after his master, doesn't he?" Jorogu said, trailing one of her delicate clawed fingers down Tony's chest.

A flush rose in his cheeks. Jorogu had been interested enough to give him the Marital Blade, but this was more than he expected.

"He just might," Tony replied with a smirk. "There's actually a couple of things I wanted to ask you about-" he started.

"My mother is going to be *so* excited to meet you, she's already started preparations for the festival, did you bring formal wear? I hope Sujuko doesn't show up, that'll be messy." Jorogu's excitement quickly shifted to a running narration of her internal monologue.

She chewed on the front knuckle of her index finger as she continued to mutter, eyes darting back and forth. Tony was no expert on Spider-People, but her face told him everything he needed to know. She was nervous, really nervous, about the whole thing, whatever it was.

This was not the Jorogu he'd crossed blades with and Tony decided that he'd remind her. He reached out and gripped the hand she'd been chewing on and pulled it away from her mouth. Her eyes shot up and met his.

"Whatever you're worried about, don't be. It's going to be alright," he said.

Tony watched the wave of relief wash over Jorogu. Her shoulders relaxed, her breathing steadied, and all tension left her face. She squeezed his hand twice rapidly and let go, her hand falling to rest on his chest again.

"Thank you, Antonious," she said, just above a whisper.

Tony smiled back at her. "One more thing, please, call me Tony," he said.

"But, is Antonious not your given name?"

"It is, but my friends call me Tony, and we're friends, right?" A coy smile crossed his face.

Flirting: Critical Success!

But I wasn't trying to-

Attribute Modifier: Clueless Flirt -1 Charisma
Note: Clueless Flirts have a 5% chance to Critically Succeed or Fail at Flirting-based Social Attacks they are unaware of making. It must be hard to be so unwittingly smooth.

"You are right, Tony, we are *at least* friends," Jorogu replied, a hint of mischief glinting in her eyes. "We must prepare you to meet Mother. Up for another climb?"

Chapter XVII: Festival Sacrament

Tony's chest heaved with effort as he tried to steady his breathing. Another three hours up the gargantuan tree and they had finally reached the Yokai Cluster's section.

Congratulations! You have reached Level 13!
Strength, Endurance, and Spirit increased by 1!
You have Unspent Attribute Points!
You have Unspent Skill Points!
You may select 1 Talent!

"Are you ready to continue?" Jorogu asked. Tony met her gaze and reciprocated the smirk she wore.

She's getting a real kick out of this, he thought.

"Just a minute and I'll be ready," he replied. Tony decided now was as good a time as any to round out some of the gaps in his build.

He hadn't interacted with anyone in a non-combat sense other than Auren since he arrived and it looked like the "clueless flirt" trait was going to get him in some trouble if he didn't do something to balance it out.

Between the points he had leftover and the points from his new level in Dread Knight, Tony's Strength, Endurance, and Spirit hit new modifier thresholds. His muscles and lungs felt fuller and despite the Saga and everything else crashing down on him, Tony was happy to be here.

Character Sheet

Name: Antonious King   Race: Human (Ascendant)

Essence: 2 (Dormant)

Class: Squire (5) | Knight (5) | Dread Knight (3)

Attributes

Strength: 20   Charisma: 14   Intelligence: 12

Dexterity: 14   Wisdom: 12   Wits: 13

Endurance: 20   Spirit: 20   Luck: 10

Skills

Melee – 10   Awareness – 5   Occult – 5

Survival – 3+   Fortitude – 10

Athletics (Freerunning) – 5

Socialize - 5

Tandem Tactics: (5)

Sagas:

Active Saga: War Against Heaven

Backgrounds:

Artifact: Pauldron of Vengeance   Familiar: Maximus

Talents

Summon Dreadblade (Life-Biting Essence)   Berserker's Stance

Pommel Strike   *New* Punishing Parry

Oath   Charge

Invincible Will   Fatal Resolve   Adamant Slash

Punishing Parry would be an excellent addition for his build, especially since he'd been in three duels in just about as many days.

Punishing Parry	
Cost: +5 Lore (10 Lore Pommel Strike)	Duration: Instant
Blunt Damage: Average	Cooldown: None
Effect: Successfully parrying an attack (Defense Rating vs. Attack Rating) with more than 5 threshold allows the Dread Knight to reflexively lash out with a Pommel Strike, interrupting their foe's offense.	

Tony nodded, dismissing his character sheet. "Alright, I'm ready. Where to next?"

Jorogu pointed to the inside of the platform. "My cluster's stores are that way, though any proper clothing that we have would need to be altered to accommodate your..." She paused for a moment, looking Tony up and down, "form," she finished. The mark on Tony's arm grew warm as she looked him over. He'd have to ask Jorogu what *she* got from the mark.

Tony walked beside the beautiful spider-woman on the wood and web platform. Jorogu's spider legs had not made another appearance since they'd met up, even during the climb. Jorogu's posture was perfect and her stride held a captivating grace.

To anyone else, her movements appeared natural and made without thought, but the tics Tony noticed at the corners of her eyes and mouth told him that being restricted to two legs was uncomfortable.

Tony racked his brain; he was sure that being seen with a human in a spider cluster came with its own pressure, but to do so while ignoring your own natural movements to make that human comfortable?

He wanted, no, needed to find a way to alleviate some of the awkwardness she had to be feeling.

"You know, back where I'm from, a lot of guys would be intimidated if their potential mate was taller than they were. I always thought that was kind of silly. Is there anything like that among your people?" Tony asked.

Jorogu paused for a moment. "Most of the mating happens early in our evolution. Males are only capable of expressing either fear or arousal at that stage. I suppose more express fear when the female is larger," she answered.

Tony nodded. "Well, if you weren't using your other legs to make me comfortable, I don't want you to worry about it," he blurted.

Jorogu blushed.

"Thank you, Tony," she said. With a gentle hiss, the eight additional legs emerged from the small of Jorogu's back.

The way Jorogu shook out her legs reminded Tony of a woman letting her hair down in a shampoo commercial.

Tony felt like he was seeing Jorogu for the first time, truly in her element; she was about a foot taller than him now, suspended in air, regal yet delicate, fierce but tender, and breathtaking all at the same time. "It would be best if we get you ready for the Festival," she said gesturing to an impressive structure of branches, leaves, and webbing.

You have received Event-Related Equipment!
(Equipment bonuses will lose potency after event period)

Festival Formal Wear (Combat)
Helmet: Doomed King's Helm (Hidden) | +10 Defense Rating
Neck: Amulet of the Promised | +0 Defense Rating
Chest: Yokai Cluster Kimono | +6 Defense Rating
Shoulders: Yokai Cluster Kataginu | +2 Defense Rating
Wrist: Yokai Cluster Bracers | +4 Defense Rating
Rings: Empty
Hands: Yokai Dueling Gloves | +2 Defense Rating
Waist: Yokai Cluster Obi | +3 Defense Rating
Legs: Yokai Cluster Hakama | +6 Defense Rating
Feet: Yokai Cluster Wajari, Tabi, Sunetae | +6 Defense Rating

Tony shuffled in the samurai-esque garments for a moment before Jorogu rested her hand on his back. She was wearing a snug, but elegant Yutaka with vibrant web and leaf motifs stitched into the artfully woven silk.

Jorogu would seem to glide across from place to place if it weren't for the spider legs holding her feet barely just above the platform.

In the time they'd spent together, mostly getting Tony into the formal wear, the pair had found a happy medium between Jorogu's comfort and the expected "perceptions" held by the Arach court.

Jorogu's arachnid appendages were spread wide and would hold her at mere inches taller than being on two feet, and as she had explained, Tony needed to appear taller than Jorogu, especially if Sujuko made an appearance. She'd explained just how important it was that the festival went off without incident when she helped him into the awkward formalwear.

"Sujuko was my first Promised One," Tony realized that when Jorogu was anxious she immediately took to chewing on the top knuckle of her index finger, which she had been as soon as Tony asked who Sujuko was.

"The Arach people's evolution is a bit one-sided when it comes to gender. Males seldom evolve to the Arachne state, they develop the same sentience any of us would, but the humanoid shape does not suit our males."

"So, does their evolution just stop?"

"In complexity, yes. The... what did you call them, 'Rally' spiders? Those are adolescents. Their fathers protect our borders and are larger than the ship you arrived in. You were fortunate to have landed where you did." Tony let the thought of a spider bigger than a condo sink in for a moment before shaking it off.

"Do I have to worry about a starship-sized ex coming after me tonight?" Tony asked with a smirk. He held up what he could best describe as a satin loincloth and looked to Jorogu, confused.

She suppressed a laugh and nodded, pointing to the loincloth and pants as she explained,

"No, not at all, Sujuko was the first male to evolve beyond the Arachne state in recorded history. Some of our fiercest warriors *did* reach Arachne, but he was the first to reach what we call the Daimyo state."

"And the Daimyo state is where you are?" Tony asked, stripping down to his boxers.

The battle-worn leather peeled away from his skin and was quickly snatched up by spiderling attendants for repair and cleaning.

Jorogu blushed and turned away. "Yes, the only way to ascend past the Daimyo state is to become King or Queen of the Arach. That secret is known only to my mother," she said, only turning back when she heard the splash of Tony entering the bath in the dressing parlor. She couldn't help but laugh watching Tony fend off a wave of spiderlings wielding scrub brushes.

"So, what should I expect?" Tony asked, surrendering to the small swarm of attendants.

"We will be expected at the Festival as a couple, you will meet my mother Semiramis, and she will set forth the challenge to consecrate our engagement." The casual tone of her explanation floored Tony.

"Consecrate our?" Tony let the question hang.

Jorogu wrung her hands and stared at them. "Our engagement. Mother is aging and for another queen to be crowned she must have a mate."

"You must be under a lot of pressure," Tony said.

"Mother forced me to promise myself to Sujuko. He had been kind, at first, but the idea of becoming King made him cruel and obsessive. I took my cluster and left nearly a year ago to 'secure' our borders to avoid the very festival we will be attending. Sujuko did not *earn* the right to be engaged, I decided that I would only be promised to one that could best me in combat, and then I found you." Tears breached the corners of her eyes and streamed down her cheeks.

The breath caught in Tony's chest. *What do I do?*

"I know that being a human and me being what I am, it-" Tony stood from the bath, spiderlings still clinging to his flesh and scrubbing away. Jorogu gasped, surprised at Tony's sudden and very naked advance.

"What are you doing?" she asked.

Tony bent down and wrapped his arms around the woman and lifted her to her feet. "Hugging you," he answered.

"So you're not..."

"Not what?"

"Disgusted by me? Angry at me?" Her extra sets of eyes scanned Tony's face while her main pair bored into his collarbone.

Tony dipped his head and chuckled into the soft waves of her hair. "No and no. You are the furthest thing from disgusting I've seen and I get it, I think. Being forced into a marriage or being bound to someone against your will must feel terrible. I don't hold the sudden, uh... proposal against you." She looked up and met Tony's gaze.

"You don't?"

Tony placed his right hand on Jorogu's cheek and kissed her, cradling her head in his hand. He pulled back and smiled at her. "Does that answer your question?"

Tony had just met the fourth noble couple when his focus returned to the present. Jorogu had been guiding him through both the literal and figurative swarm of Arachne nobility.

None of them spoke English as well as Jorogu, but they were able to navigate conversation easily enough. The crowd parted and Jorogu squeezed Tony's bicep as Semiramis approached.

She held herself at the full height allowed by her thick and wicked arachnid appendages; the resemblance between mother and daughter was uncanny, save for a few distinct differences. The cascades of her translucent ashen hair were pinned up in eloquent interlocking loops, and her skin lacked the same near pink flush that Jorogu's held, but maintained the same soft appearance, everything about her radiated royalty.

"You must be the human, my daughter's Promised. Antonius?" she said, her voice was sagacious.

Semiramis only asks questions that she knows the answers to, Jorogu had told him.

Tony bowed low from the waist, not taking his eyes from the Queen. "I am, majesty. I am Antonious King."

"You may stand, boy, let me get a good look at you," the Queen said, lowering herself to be eye level with Tony.

He stood perfectly still as the matriarch circled and examined him. She prodded at his muscles, listened to his heartbeat, and stared into his eyes. Tony steeled himself, he knew that if Semiramis saw, heard, or felt something that she didn't like he was as good as dead. She clicked and whistled a fair number of times; Tony had to hide his surprise when he understood what was said.

Your Intelligence has increased!

You have learned a new Language: Arach - Basic

"Not bad, advanced musculature for a human, a strong heart, this soul, however..." The Queen's eyes blazed with viridian light, and her gaze intensified, boring into his. Tony felt a pressure building up in the center of his torso, a roiling angry mass, squirming under scrutiny. It was familiar to him, this raging smear on his soul. It was the same *thing* that had taken hold of him after he had rescued Maximus. Tony harnessed his will and forced it at the smear, forcing it down and away.

Semiramis's eyes dimmed and a wry smile crossed her face. "You have some demons to reconcile, boy, fortunately for you, I don't trust a man without a dark side."

Tony let out a relieved sigh. "Thank you, highness."

"Now, for your challenge, should you truly seek my daughter Jorogu's hand-"

Startled gasps came from the entrance to the hall, accompanied by belligerent shouting. Semiramis rolled her eyes and stretched back to her full height. "Is about to arrive, it would seem."

A shot of adrenaline coursed through Tony's body as a giant of a man somersaulted over his head and landed between him and Semiramis.

"I assert my rite as Promised One to challenge this interloper for Jorogu's hand!" He was at least eight feet tall, not including the gravity-defying spikes of blood-red hair and the appendages sprouting from his shoulders, poised like serpents ready to strike above him.

Why do they always have to be so much bigger than me? Tony lamented.

"Get to it then, Sujuko. I will not have the festival interrupted any further," the Queen answered. She clacked her forelegs together three times and the swarm cleared to form a ring, Tony, Sujuko, Jorogu, and Semiramis at its center. "As the challenged, you are to set the terms," Semiramis said, gesturing to Tony. "We would hear them now."

"We will duel to satisfaction to be determined by you, highness. I have no other conditions." Tony's voice came out harder than he meant; he ignored the surprise that flashed across Sujuko's face and glared into the man's eyes.

he evening sky glowed like a ruddy afternoon
a pillar of light struck Sujuko. He grew to ten
eight, the legs of burning essence dimmed and
shed as molten articulated steel formed over
ch ending in a serrated blade and bringing his
o count well over twenty.

wave of essence rolled over Tony and the
s Sujuko's roar pierced the night sky, chasing
e molten essence and light.

Are you ready for round two, Ascendant?" the
growled.

nough!" Semiramis shouted, shaking the
with her decree, her eyes blazing with beryl
declare this duel finished! And you, Sujuko,
out from this cluster! Combat under the
e or power of another is strictly forbidden and
our laws. Now leave, before I summon your
o remove you!" The viridian sheen in the
eyes was extinguished as swiftly as it had
ed as a spike the size of a ballista bolt took her
the chest and pinned her to the far wall.

've had enough of your prattling," Sujuko
as the molten glow of essence receded, his
shot leg growing back and coating with the
netal.

"I find these terms acceptable," Sujuko yelled; he pumped his arms and flexed his arachnid appendages.

He's posturing. Tony ground his teeth and took two steps back. He didn't have time for theatrics. Jorogu squeezed his shoulder and moved to "ringside."

Semiramis looked between Tony and Sujuko, each nodded in response to the silent question of readiness.

"Begin!" she commanded.

You are in Combat

Tony surged at the massive man, ignoring the awkwardness of movement in the formalwear. Sujuko sneered at him and braced, prepared to meet Tony's seemingly unarmed charge.

The instant before they collided, Tony dropped into a slide and shot between the goliath's legs. Sujuko was surprised but showed alarming reflexes as he wheeled around, lashing out with his trunk-like arm and spear-length appendages. Tony drew the Marital Blade and held it flat against his shoulder, absorbing the blow and sending him sliding back.

Jorogu's Marital Blade
Rarity: Unique (1 of 1) Durability: 97% Enchantments: Unyielding, Dueling
Slashing Damage: Exceptional Thrusting Damage: Good
Parry: Good Riposte Multiplier: 3.75x
Unyielding: The wielder does not know surrender and gains +5% Attack and Defense Rating for every 10% of missing HP Dueling: The wielder gains +20% Attack Rating and +20% to Defense Rating (Parry) when in combat against 1 foe

Sujuko's eyes went wide before narrowing in a jealous rage. "You *dare* dishonor me by using *that* to fight me? Very well!" He stretched his arms high overhead as the spider legs protruding from his shoulders interlocked and calcified to form a colossal great-axe.

Tony's lips drew back in a snarl. "Compensating for something?"

Sujuko roared in response and hurtled forward, the wicked axe held high overhead.

"So predictable," Tony muttered as he sidestepped the overhead swing and swatted the back of the weapon, burying the blade in the ground and triggering Punishing Parry. He slammed the pommel of the sword into the underside of the giant's chin, sending him reeling and clutching his face.

Tony had two secor damage as possible while adl duel. He slammed the sw ground and slammed his fist and neck; Tony's growl of eff cry as he continued his assaul

Punishing Parry's stu hands blurred in among his Tony's onslaught and abandc

In deflecting the telegraphed counter punches of those landing would hurt

He shifted his stance jabs that forced Sujuko to followed him like a sha advantage, attacking the m fists and feet slammed int armpits, biceps, neck, an stabilizing muscles would m slow and off-balance, from t apart until the duel was calle

Combat Statu
Dire Battle – XP increased by 25 defeat

"Oh, shit." Tony leape of burning golden light tear and searing the flesh on his r

storm feet in exting them, total li

crowd away

monst

groun flame. are ca influer agains father Queen blosson throug

growle recentl vicious

Tony's instincts screamed in alarm as he pitched himself to the right, the spike aimed at his face whistling past his ear instead before plunging through the members of the court behind him, viscera and ichor in its wake.

"What will it be, Ascendant? Continue to run away, and allow those behind you to die, or stand and fight like a man!" the beast taunted.

What do I do? They're too fast, but more of Jorogu's people will die if I dodge them.

Tony squared his stance and held the Marital Blade in front of him. The people behind him were already dead, and if he could endure a couple of hits, he could probably figure out the timing and pattern.

"Good man," Sujuko said, firing a spike.

Tony swatted it aside and screamed in pain as two more pierced his shoulders and pinned him to the floor.

"Fuck," Tony groaned. Fifty percent of his HP was gone, and he doubted that Sujuko would only be firing one spike at a time, which wouldn't give him the chance to activate Fatal Resolve.

"That Marital Blade is as good as mine, mortal." The ground shook with every step the mammoth took toward him.

"ΜΟΛΩΝ ΛΑΒΕ, motherfucker," Tony growled.

The Doomed King's Helm materialized in place and Tony reached up for one of the spikes pinning him in place.

MOΛΩN ΛABE - Defense Rating vs Ranged Attacks increased by 20%

Getting free of one of them might do enough damage to activate Fatal Resolve, then he could free himself from the other and get back in the fight. His blood froze when Sujuko's footfalls stopped and the sound of steel crashing against steel reached his ears.

"You will not have him!" Jorogu shouted, pushing the tempo of battle.

Get up! You have to get up! Tony pushed against the floor, sliding slowly up the spikes. *Just a few more seconds!*

Jorogu's body soared overhead, a spike through her abdomen. A sensation of cold seared through him from the mark on his arm.

His eyes followed Jorogu and fixed on where she landed.

She wasn't breathing.

"I find these terms acceptable," Sujuko yelled; he pumped his arms and flexed his arachnid appendages.

He's posturing. Tony ground his teeth and took two steps back. He didn't have time for theatrics. Jorogu squeezed his shoulder and moved to "ringside."

Semiramis looked between Tony and Sujuko, each nodded in response to the silent question of readiness.

"Begin!" she commanded.

> You are in Combat

Tony surged at the massive man, ignoring the awkwardness of movement in the formalwear. Sujuko sneered at him and braced, prepared to meet Tony's seemingly unarmed charge.

The instant before they collided, Tony dropped into a slide and shot between the goliath's legs. Sujuko was surprised but showed alarming reflexes as he wheeled around, lashing out with his trunk-like arm and spear-length appendages. Tony drew the Marital Blade and held it flat against his shoulder, absorbing the blow and sending him sliding back.

Jorogu's Marital Blade
Rarity: Unique (1 of 1)   Durability: 97% Enchantments: Unyielding, Dueling
Slashing Damage: Exceptional   Thrusting Damage: Good
Parry: Good   Riposte Multiplier: 3.75x
Unyielding: The wielder does not know surrender and gains +5% Attack and Defense Rating for every 10% of missing HP Dueling: The wielder gains +20% Attack Rating and +20% to Defense Rating (Parry) when in combat against 1 foe

Sujuko's eyes went wide before narrowing in a jealous rage. "You *dare* dishonor me by using *that* to fight me? Very well!" He stretched his arms high overhead as the spider legs protruding from his shoulders interlocked and calcified to form a colossal great-axe.

Tony's lips drew back in a snarl. "Compensating for something?"

Sujuko roared in response and hurtled forward, the wicked axe held high overhead.

"So predictable," Tony muttered as he sidestepped the overhead swing and swatted the back of the weapon, burying the blade in the ground and triggering Punishing Parry. He slammed the pommel of the sword into the underside of the giant's chin, sending him reeling and clutching his face.

Tony had two seconds to inflict as much damage as possible while adhering to the tenets of the duel. He slammed the sword point-first into the ground and slammed his fists into Sujuko's chest, gut, and neck; Tony's growl of effort blossomed into a war cry as he continued his assault.

Punishing Parry's stun wore off and Sujuko's hands blurred in among his own attempting to deflect Tony's onslaught and abandoning his axe.

In deflecting the mammoth man-spider's telegraphed counter punches; Tony could tell that one of those landing would hurt tremendously.

He shifted his stance after landing a series of jabs that forced Sujuko to break engagement and followed him like a shadow and pressed the advantage, attacking the man's soft targets. Tony's fists and feet slammed into Sujuko's inner thighs, armpits, biceps, neck, and groin. Disabling the stabilizing muscles would make his opponent's attacks slow and off-balance, from there Tony could pick him apart until the duel was called in his favor.

Combat Status Changed
Dire Battle – XP increased by 25% – Final Death will occur if defeated

"Oh, shit." Tony leaped back, spider legs made of burning golden light tearing through his Kataginu and searing the flesh on his right shoulder.

The evening sky glowed like a ruddy afternoon storm as a pillar of light struck Sujuko. He grew to ten feet in height, the legs of burning essence dimmed and extinguished as molten articulated steel formed over them, each ending in a serrated blade and bringing his total limb count well over twenty.

A wave of essence rolled over Tony and the crowd as Sujuko's roar pierced the night sky, chasing away the molten essence and light.

"Are you ready for round two, Ascendant?" the monster growled.

"Enough!" Semiramis shouted, shaking the ground with her decree, her eyes blazing with beryl flame. "I declare this duel finished! And you, Sujuko, are cast out from this cluster! Combat under the influence or power of another is strictly forbidden and against our laws. Now leave, before I summon your father to remove you!" The viridian sheen in the Queen's eyes was extinguished as swiftly as it had blossomed as a spike the size of a ballista bolt took her through the chest and pinned her to the far wall.

"I've had enough of your prattling," Sujuko growled as the molten glow of essence receded, his recently shot leg growing back and coating with the vicious metal.

Tony's instincts screamed in alarm as he pitched himself to the right, the spike aimed at his face whistling past his ear instead before plunging through the members of the court behind him, viscera and ichor in its wake.

"What will it be, Ascendant? Continue to run away, and allow those behind you to die, or stand and fight like a man!" the beast taunted.

What do I do? They're too fast, but more of Jorogu's people will die if I dodge them.

Tony squared his stance and held the Marital Blade in front of him. The people behind him were already dead, and if he could endure a couple of hits, he could probably figure out the timing and pattern.

"Good man," Sujuko said, firing a spike.

Tony swatted it aside and screamed in pain as two more pierced his shoulders and pinned him to the floor.

"Fuck," Tony groaned. Fifty percent of his HP was gone, and he doubted that Sujuko would only be firing one spike at a time, which wouldn't give him the chance to activate Fatal Resolve.

"That Marital Blade is as good as mine, mortal." The ground shook with every step the mammoth took toward him.

"ΜΟΛΩΝ ΛΑΒΕ, motherfucker," Tony growled.

The Doomed King's Helm materialized in place and Tony reached up for one of the spikes pinning him in place.

MOΛΩN ΛABE - Defense Rating vs Ranged Attacks increased by 20%

Getting free of one of them might do enough damage to activate Fatal Resolve, then he could free himself from the other and get back in the fight. His blood froze when Sujuko's footfalls stopped and the sound of steel crashing against steel reached his ears.

"You will not have him!" Jorogu shouted, pushing the tempo of battle.

Get up! You have to get up! Tony pushed against the floor, sliding slowly up the spikes. *Just a few more seconds!*

Jorogu's body soared overhead, a spike through her abdomen. A sensation of cold seared through him from the mark on his arm.

His eyes followed Jorogu and fixed on where she landed.

She wasn't breathing.

Chapter XVIII: Ascendant: Online

Tony's chest burned with rage.

He'd come here to get away from the whole "Celestial being trying to kill him" thing and instead he'd brought the conflict with him. Jorogu and her people had paid for it.

"You son of a bitch, you came here to fight for her, now look! She's not moving!" One of the spikes snapped off, putting Tony on one knee. He used the Marital Blade to cleave through the other and got to his feet.

Sujuko wasn't looking too hot, most of his launchable legs were gone and not growing back and the fact that he wasn't firing at Tony right away meant that he probably wasn't sure if they'd grow back at all.

The anger burning in Tony was unlike any he had ever felt. The bottled-up regret, angst, self-loathing, and sorrow had burst open and mixed with the absolute fury and contempt he held for the "man" standing before him.

His heart pounded like a war drum, every muscle in his body drew taut, his vision scored red; there was only one thing left to do.

Tony surged forward with such force that the platform turned up and shattered in his wake, the surprise on Sujuko's face only grew as Tony's fist sent him soaring back thirty feet. The monster got to his feet only to receive Tony's dropkick into his gut sending him face-first into the platform.

"Come on, get up!" Tony bellowed. He stalked toward the man-spider, Marital Blade held loosely by his side. Sujuko shot up and launched three of his remaining spikes at Tony.

They were so easy for him to follow.

Tony deflected two of them with an upward slash and lodged the tip of his blade into the third, swinging it around the entirety of his body before flinging the spike off and back at Sujuko with a shout.

The beast weaved to the side and caught the spike, twirled it in his grip, and dropped into a low stance holding it out in front of him like a spear.

Pure bloodlust nearly boiled over when a cough snapped Tony out of his frenzy. For a moment, he thought, he hoped, it was Jorogu. Semiramis emerged from a pile of wreckage and bodies, arms extended and spinnerets spewing webbing at Sujuko, rooting him in place. She locked eyes with Tony, her gaze a blazing emerald bonfire.

"Fight him in anger and you will fall. You must think beyond the moment," she commanded.

Tony took deep ragged breaths. The tempest of emotions made focusing difficult, Semiramis was right, if he couldn't regain a center Tony would be fighting not only Sujuko but himself.

"Quickly, Antonious, I cannot hold him for long," Semiramis called.

Tony went to do what he always did and pull his emotions in and bottle them, but the bottle was broken, there was nowhere to keep them. Instead, he forced them outward, making a storm wall and Tony the eye of the tempest. His eyes snapped open in the same moment Sujuko broke free and Semiramis ran out of webbing.

The beast rushed forward and Tony moved to intercept. Their exchange was rapid staccato clashes of steel on steel. Tony lost himself in the rhythm of the fight, moving seamlessly from offense to defense and back again.

He didn't think, he just moved. Sujuko's grunts of pain, flashes of ichor, and burning light were the only indication that the balance of the fight was tipping.

For every cut Tony made, molten essence poured out and scarred over at near-instant speeds; the "gift" of regeneration given to Sujuko by Ignacious seemed to be draining his total "pool" of Essence, keeping his HP up while failing to generate additional spikes, spider legs, or weaponry.

He couldn't let up, if Sujuko had enough time to reload Tony would be in trouble.

Tony redoubled his efforts, thrusting and cutting away at his foe when the hair on the back of his neck stood up on end. It was the same feeling when Sujuko got his first boost from Ignacious.

Another one, really? Can't he try to kill someone else?

Tony dropped a pommel strike in the middle of Sujuko's chest, caving it in. The beast dropped his javelin and hunched forward, gasping for air. Tony used the back of Sujuko's neck like a springboard, soaring above him and intercepting the incoming boost.

You Have Unlocked an Achievement!

What's not Mine is also Mine!

Steal a Power-up or piece of High-Rarity Loot from an enemy

Traits have Awakened!

Essence (Awakened)

Ascendant Healing Factor

Ascendant Attribute Enhancement

Congratulations, You have Ascended

The rush of power that flowed through Tony was intoxicating, the remnants of the spikes in his shoulders popped out and the holes burned closed shortly after. Tony's eyes flashed to his status bar as a buff flashed at him:

Throes of Ascension
Essence Trait increased to 8
Duration: 29s

He could *feel* the Essence around him, how to manipulate it, weaponize it, *use it.* Tony flexed his will and sprung from the Essence in the air behind him launching down at Sujuko.

It was time to end this.

The Marital Blade clashed against all three of the spikes Sujuko brought up to meet Tony's attack. Sparks flew in every direction. Even with the boost from his Ascension and the stolen buff, he needed more. Tony growled, straining against Sujuko's defense. Maximus and his Dreadblade were back in the lounge he'd dressed and bathed in.

I guess it doesn't really matter anymore.

Tony roared and activated Adamant Slash; the indigo essence thrummed and pulsed through his weapon with a high-pitched whine and bisected the gargantuan man-spider.

Jorogu's Marital Blade		
Rarity: Unique (1 of 1) Durability: 13% Enchantments: Unyielding, Dueling (N/A Durability Low)		
Slashing Damage: Exceptional Thrusting Damage: Good		
Parry: Good Riposte Multiplier: 3.75x		

The top two-thirds of the blade shattered into gleaming shards, embedding themselves into what remained of Sujuko's body.

Tony stood over the corpse, frustrated. He wanted to *do* something, send a message. Sujuko was dead and further aggression wouldn't do anything to ease his mind.

"Antonious, come here," Semiramis croaked, the effort of the conflict glaringly obvious on her withering frame.

Her cheeks and eyes were sunken and pallid, the skin across the entirety of her body grew wan and taut. The Queen was dying.

Tony rushed to her side and caught her toppling body in his arms. "How can I help? What do you need?" he rattled.

"I need you to save Jorogu," she said.

Tony opened his mouth to answer, but nothing came out. His throat slammed shut and his eyes stung with tears. He hadn't known Jorogu for long at all. She was a *good* person who wanted to live her life and choose who she would love, not be forced into an arranged marriage for the sake of the bloodline.

"She's gone..." he managed.

"Says you, who know so much of our people?" the Queen chided, a wry smirk crossing her fading features. "I know where you are from, the technology your people hold. You... We can save her, Antonious."

Tony jumped as he heard Maximus's small growl and the sound of steel dragging across wood. He turned and saw the pup's rear high in the air heading toward him, the guard of Tony's Dreadblade gripped firmly in his teeth. Semiramis dug her fingers into Tony's bicep and reclaimed his attention. "Just tell me what to do, I'll do whatever it takes."

"You must take her body to your flagship and then put her in your pods. Before she is sealed inside, you must put my heart in the wound," she explained.

"How do you know about- wait, what?"

"I am the Queen of all Arach, Jorogu marked you and just as I could see through her eyes should I wish, I could see through the mark."

Tony shook his head, he couldn't get his head around the request, let alone the explanation. "I don't know-"

"There is no time for uncertainty. Take up that blade and take the heart from my chest, go back to your people, put it inside the hole in her chest, then seal her in one of your regeneration pods." Her eyes blazed viridian once more, punctuating her command.

The hilt of the Dreadblade landed in his open right hand, covered in puppy drool. "As you wish," he muttered, heaving the weapon up to his shoulder.

"One last thing, Antonious. You must do this quickly. If the Empire is without a leader for too long they will become feral, monstrous. That cannot happen."

Tony nodded in understanding. "Be done with it then, I'm ready."

You have received a Quest!
King of Hearts: To save both the sentience and people of the Arach Empire, you must perform the Rite of Rulership on behalf of the Arach Queen and her heir.
Rewards: XP, Dread Knight Set Piece, Jorogu Social Link Increase
Bonus Objective: Put Jorogu in an Ascendant Regeneration Pod within 6 hours

Tony set his jaw and plunged the Dreadblade into Semiramis's chest. She gasped, but that was it. No shout of pain, no cursing, nothing. He reached into her chest and pushed the wound open, getting a full view of the heart. Steeling his resolve, as not to vacate the contents of his stomach, he wrenched the blade back and forth, cleaving the heart out. Tony gripped the heart gently; it pumped once in his hand before going still.

Tony set the Queen's body down on the ground, crossed her arms over her chest, and closed her eyes. He went to sling the Dreadblade over his shoulder and realized that the Pauldron of Vengeance wasn't there. He opened his Equipment screen and received a prompt:

Event Period has expired, return Event Equipment and restore Previous Loadout?

Yes   No

Tony selected "Yes" and watched as his equipment changed over on its own, then sheathed his Dreadblade. When he looked for the remnants of the Marital Blade, Tony was shocked to see a bracer made of the same material clamped around his right arm, Jorogu's mark emblazoned prominently on the armor directly above the mark on his skin.

Covenant		
Rarity: Unique (1 of 2)	Durability: N/A	Armor Slot: Wrist
Type: Organic	Attack Rating Bonus: +5	Defense Rating: +5
Note: The remnants of Destroyed Item "Jorogu's Marital Blade"		
The symbol of a continued Promise		

Tony decided to look into this new armor piece later; he was on a time limit. Semiramis's Heart vanished from his hand and appeared in the "Quest Items" sub-menu of the Quest Log.

Tony squelched his curiosity before it got the better of him and closed his menus, put Maximus in the web-sling on his back, and walked over to where Jorogu's body lay.

The memory of her body soaring over him flashed to the front of his mind. Everything about this felt *wrong*.

She'd leaped to his defense when he had been helpless, she had died protecting him because her ex had buddied up with the number one douchebag in the known galaxy, and he had just carved out her mother's heart to cram where a dissolving metal spike protruded from.

He brushed the strands of mottled hair from her face. "I'm sorry. None of this would have happened if I didn't come back here. I... I should have waited until I was stronger... until I knew I could protect you." Just as the air caught in Tony's throat, Maximus, ever his emotional savior, barked and yipped and licked the back of his neck. He couldn't help but smile.

"What, boy?"

It okay! We save spooder lady with thump-thump and glow bubbles! a voice spoke into Tony's mind.

"Did you just talk to me?" Tony almost shouted, looking over his shoulder at the small dog.

I talka you allatime! You hear me now? Maximus asked.

"Yeah boy, I hear you!" Tears welled up in Tony's eyes. "I hear you."

Yay! Leggo to zoom room! I know where glow stick go!

"The access key?" Tony asked.

Yis, glow stick. Taste bad, no fun for play, his companion answered.

Tony scooped Jorogu's body up in his arms. *This is not how I imagined the Threshold Carry going,* he thought.

"Lead on, buddy!"

Chapter XIX: Level-Up

Tony swiftly learned that though Maximus was a great navigator, a pup in a backpack was easily distracted. He knelt and Maximus hopped down.

"I'll follow you, buddy. Show me where the glow stick goes!" Maximus took off like a shot and Tony sprinted after him. To his surprise and woe, he was able to keep up with the dog while carrying Jorogu's lifeless body.

Glow stick go dis way! Maximus took a sharp left and then a right, paws scrabbling on the platform, and darted into a smaller structure. Tony followed and slid to a stop behind the dog. The room was small and bereft of windows. In the center of the room, there was a "web" made of some sort of shifting metal pulsing with a rainbow of greens, purples, and yellows.

Maximus pawed at his leg. *I go on back now, please?* Tony knelt again and the dog went face-first into the sling. The small dog wriggled, tail wagging all the while until he was right-side-up in the harness.

Tony waited until Maximus had steadied himself and set Jorogu down, freeing his hands to catch the Access Key as it popped out of his inventory.

It was an odd thing to witness, a small pip of light, a popping sound and then the item appeared. Tony pushed the spike into the center of the web on a guess.

The Access Key flashed red and its light merged with the cascade of color, dancing among the other flashes of light on the walls of the small room.

Tony scooped Jorogu up and stepped onto the mercurial web. A chill shot through the soles of his boots and up through his spine as a warp map flashed in front of him. A wide array of planetary points showed on the map and one off-planet; the Haght'anak warp point was a small circle in space.

Tony selected the Flagship and would have jumped if the web hadn't held him in place. The glowing lattice sprung up from the floor and wrapped around him, pulsing with a red array light. A blast of heat surged through the room.

Tony could feel sections of the web burn away. As soon as it was gone, instead of being flung into a star, like Tony thought he would be, he found himself standing back on the warp pad of the Haght'anak.

A mob of easily thirty people stood in the warp room. As one, they turned to look at him. Selenians, Ashtar, and Celestial Elves stared at Tony and the body in his arms. Their voices all rose at once, a cacophony of questions, demands, and concern and they pushed forward, swarming him. A debuff appeared under his status bars.

Stressed
You are overwhelmed, mentally, physically, spiritually, or all of the preceding
Dexterity and Strength increased by 5
Charisma and Stamina reduced by 5
Duration: Varies
Remove yourself from the Stressor to begin Debuff Countdown

Tony didn't need to be told twice. "Pardon me, 'scuse me, please move," Tony found himself repeating over and over as he pushed through the crowd.

He heard Maximus yelp in the same instant that some grasping limb struck Tony across the face. He turned to look and saw the hands of a fire-aspected Ashtar trying to tug his dog free of the harness on his back.

"Get your hands off of him!" Tony's voice seemed to bludgeon the gaggle of recently respawned Ascendants with the unspoken "or else" its violent tone carried.

The crowd parted in front of him and Tony rushed out. He took note of the various spells being charged, weapons drawn, and arrows nocked in his direction.

Tony didn't care.

As soon as he was out of the room, the timer on his Stressed debuff began to count down, only fifteen seconds.

Tony still had a good chunk of time to get Jorogu into the tank and time to spare on the bonus objective. He leaned against the wall around a couple of corners and took a minute to breathe. Maximus joined in, panting heavily. The Ashtar that grabbed at him had scorched his fur and knocked five percent of the pup's HP off as a result.

"Are you okay, bud?" Tony asked.

Too hot hands from mean boy hurted me, the small pup whined both physically and mentally, the pitch of the whimper fanning the protective anger burning in Tony's gut.

"After we save spider-lady, do you think you could find the mean boy?"

Prob'ly, why you wanna find him? Maximus sniffed behind Tony's ear, as if searching for the answer to his question there.

"I think it would be a good idea to teach him a lesson," Tony growled.

Maximus nipped the lobe of Tony's ear and unleashed a rapid series of barks. *No! Bad daddy, no hurt peoples! Only ve'y bad peoples like can butt and were-spooder!*

Tony's eyes went wide. The dog was right, knocking some sense into a presumably low-leveled Ascendant for trying to dognap Maximus wasn't the *right* thing to do, no matter how much better he would feel in the moment after.

"Alright, buddy, alright. I won't hurt him, promise," Tony cooed.

Maximus let out a jovial yip and licked at Tony's earlobe.

As they walked to the regeneration and respawn chambers, more Ascendants walked past him, staring at the body in his arms, then at the dog on his back. In most cases, a glare sent them on their way and he could move on uninterrupted. There was one incident where his glare had nearly started a fight, but the Celestial Elf that was so quick to get in Tony's face swiftly backed down when they realized he had nearly six levels on him.

Maximus's chorus of barks and yowling accompanied by his "mental broadcast" nearly caused Tony to fall over laughing. *Yeah! Heck you, Bubby! You meanie butt! I pee in your shoes, you be mean-a my daddy again!*

"You are going to get so many treats when I have free hands, bud."

Having finally arrived at the Regeneration Pods, Tony lowered Jorogu's legs to the floor and held the rest of her up against him. Her body was cold to the touch, but when it came into full contact with his, it grew warm and trembled. He looked down at Jorogu's face, hoping to see her eyes opened, looking back at him with that shy smile splashed across her lips.

No such luck.

Tony pressed his palm against the panel to the right of the pod and it hissed open. He stepped half inside and stood Jorogu against the back wall. Wires and sensor pads shot out from seemingly nowhere and fastened to her. Tony fought back the urge to tear them off, they would help, he was sure.

Concentrating on his quest items, Semiramis's heart appeared in his hand. Tony peeled back the tattered Yutaka covering Jorogu's chest wound. Despite having seen underneath the Yutaka in the bathhouse, the act made Tony uncomfortable, but not nearly as uncomfortable as what he had to do next.

Gritting his teeth, Tony pushed the Queen's heart into Jorogu's open chest. The organ immediately pumped, writhing in his grip. Tony withdrew his hand, eyes wide as he watched arteries and veins sprout from the Queen's heart and splice into Jorogu's.

"Regeneration Pod Activated. Sealing in ten seconds," the ship's AI spoke. Tony stepped out of the pod and watched the door slide up, mere inches ahead of the roiling blue-green regeneration fluid.

You have Completed a Quest!

King of Hearts: To save both the sentience and people of the Arach Empire, you must perform the Rite of Rulership on behalf of the Arach Queen and her heir.

Bonus Objective Completed! As a result, 3 Derangements (Jorogu) have been subverted!

Bonus XP Awarded!

Witness the Beginning

Congratulations, you have reached Level 14!

Congratulations, you have reached Level 15!

You have 3 Unspent Talent Points

You Have Unspent Skill Points

You have Unspent Attribute Points

Your Ascendant Attribute Enhancement Bonus is Available!

Ascendant Class Options have been Unlocked!

You may Select a Dread Knight Set Piece

Shards of Brísingamen
Rarity: Unique   Durability: 100%   Armor Slot: Neck Type: Artifact
Remnants of the fabled "Gleaming Torc" Shards of Brísingamen holds two minor Enchantments
Fire Immunity (Minor): Functions as Greater Fire Resistance
Greater Fire Resistance: Damage from Natural Fire-Based Attacks reduced by 80%, Damage from Magical Fire-Based Attacks reduced by 40%, can withstand extreme Hot Weather for up to 20160 minutes before penalties for overexposure and heat-based damage apply.

Gjöll Stone Amulet
Rarity: Unique   Durability: 100%   Armor Slot: Neck Type: Artifact
A carved piece of Magma harvested from the riverbank of Gjöll at the onset of Ragnarök. It is said that this amulet holds the unbound essence of the great Flame-Wolf. Only time will tell.
Effect: Unknown

Your Social Link with Jorogu has Increased!

Social Rank: 6   Status: Betrothed

Through your actions, your devotion toward this person is unparalleled. Your status is widely known through the Arach Empire, its allies, and its enemies.

Tony winced at the last phrase of the Social Link notification. He had no doubts that an empire would have political enemies, especially after the mention of border security and how the males evolved into engines of destruction. What enemies did the Arach Empire have? Were there Lizard or Bird people out there? Another colony of Spider-people with conflicting views?

As fascinating as it was to think about, Tony didn't have the time to do so at his leisure. There was a God who wanted him dead and had the means to power up his enemies from seemingly anywhere, even without the "avatar" he used to try and kill him being present.

Tony selected the Gjöll Stone Amulet and opened his sheet to spend his remaining points, only to be gobsmacked at the full gravity of what "Ascension" had done to his stats. All of his attributes had increased by **five points**, on top of that, fifteen was clearly a milestone level. The extra attribute points he had to spend on top of what was there left him giddy.

There was one customization to his Dread Knight class that he had to make before continuing.

> Please select an Ascendant Specialization before continuing

Dread Knight - Blademaster Ascension
This specialization of the Dread Knight class enhances the Dread Knight's capabilities with their Dreadblade at the cost of advanced spell casting.

Dread Knight - Spellblade Ascension
This specialization of the Dread Knight class enhances the Dread Knight's spell casting capacity, granting them an Arcane Focus and spell slots equal to half of their total level in an Arcane Magic Class of their choice. Precludes advanced Martial Talents.

Dread Knight - Death's Triumphant Ascension
This specialization of the Dread Knight class enhances the Dread Knight's survival. Upon death, the Dread Knight respawns as a Shade of incredible power for 48 hours. If the Dread Knight does not return to the site of their demise, Death comes to claim them permanently. All second-wind talents and healing talents are refunded and precluded from purchase.

As tempting as picking up a bunch of spells for free and being semi-immortal was, Tony wasn't willing to sacrifice the Advanced Martial Talents; he was going to need those to kill Ignacious. On top of that, shades could be targeted by holy magic and easily destroyed and even though the pitfalls of Fatal Resolve had been very clearly indicated, he'd rather have it than lose it. He selected the Blademaster Ascension and moved through the rest of his upgrades.

Character Sheet

Name: Antonious King   Race: Ascendant   Essence: 3

Class: Squire (5) | Knight (5) | Dread Knight [Blademaster] (5)

Attributes

Strength: 25   Charisma: 20   Intelligence: 20

Dexterity: 20   Wisdom: 20   Wits: 20

Endurance: 25   Spirit: 25   Luck: 15

Skills

Melee – 20   Awareness – 10   Occult – 10

Survival – 5   Fortitude – 15   Athletics (Freerunning) – 10

Socialize - 5   Tandem Tactics: (5)   Resolve: 5

Sagas:

Active Saga: War Against Heaven

Backgrounds:

Artifact: Pauldron of Vengeance   Covenant   Gjöll
Stone Amulet

Familiar: Maximus

Talents

Summon Dreadblade (Life-Biting Essence)

Berserker's Stance   Frenzied Blood Rapture *new*

Pommel Strike   Punishing Parry

Oath   Charge

Invincible Will+ *new*

Fatal Resolve   Adamant Slash

Bloody Haste *new*

Frenzied Blood Rapture was a straightforward upgrade over Berserker's Stance, removing the killing condition on stamina regeneration and replacing it with "wounding" enemies who would grant experience when defeated.

Invincible Will+ now added a twenty percent boost to Strength when attempting to break free of physical bonds in addition to the mental compulsion.

Bloody Haste was something else.

Bloody Haste		
Cost: 10% HP	Duration: 30 seconds	Cooldown: 2 minutes
Effect: Gain thirty percent Haste on Activation, Reduce Cooldown on inactive Talents		

It was the first traditional "cooldown" Tony had unlocked; level fifteen was certainly the milestone it had been laid out to be. He remembered reading about World of Warcraft's raids and how there would be three bosses per "wing" of the raid and using all of their encounter-based cooldowns to save time as they would be ready to use by the time the next boss fight came.

Maximus's head plopped down onto Tony's shoulder, the pup was exhausted and now that Tony took a second to evaluate, he was too. It had been at *least* four days since Tony's head hit a pillow. Everything else could wait at least four hours.

Tony traced the first steps he took into the hangar back to the room he woke up in. The room was, fortunately, untouched. He reached over his shoulder and placed Maximus on the ground. The pup perked up for a moment, tail wagging.

"You ready for a nap, bud?"

Maximus let out a low "woof" and jumped straight from the floor into the bed. Tony peeled off his armor, content to drop it on the floor, and climbed into bed. Maximus shuffled under the covers and curled against Tony's chest and let out a deep sigh.

Sleep claimed them both swiftly, and without mercy.

Chapter XX: Brink

"You were a loser! A nobody! I made you a warrior, *Antonious,* do you think you would have made it to where you are now without me?" Bruce shouted.

"That's just typical, Bruce! You may have put me through Hell, but *I'm the one* who fought through all of it! Where do you get off taking credit for *any* of it?" Tony bellowed back.

"You got your first black belt in sixth grade, got into your first fistfight in sixth grade, and won. Do you think that would have happened if I hadn't pushed you? Those boys would have killed you!"

Spittle flew from Bruce's mouth as his face turned the deep scarlet that foreshadowed a rant. "Then your Freshman year, those six thugs that were going to mug you, the officer thought you were *lying* about beating them all half to death. Kendo, you're welcome. You wanted to quit after the first week and *I didn't let you!*"

Tony's heart pounded against his ribs. His chest swelled with rage and anxiety, he hated it when Bruce got like this.

Always during tournament season, always when Tony didn't want to compete, Bruce's attempts at persuading him had gone from placating Tony to guilt trips, and now to this, playing on his need to prove Bruce wrong. This time Tony knew. This time it wouldn't work.

"So what? Maybe I wish those thugs *did* kill me? Maybe I wanted to lose?" Tony shot back.

Bruce was unfazed. "Oh, c'mon son, you're just saying that because of the dog-"

"SHUT UP!" Tony shoved Bruce into the kitchen island, right fist cocked, and violence in his eyes.

Bruce swung the brass bowl, recently vacated of its fruit, at Tony's face. Tony ducked, tucking both arms to his sides, and slammed his left fist into Bruce's side. It felt like punching a steel beam. A fist the size of a cinderblock streaked toward Tony like a falling comet. He weaved to the right.

If you're gonna get hit, you're gonna get hit. You pick where, Scott's voice echoed.

Bruce's fist impacted with Tony's left shoulder, dislocating it and propelling Tony's right hook into his square jaw. Both combatants staggered back.

"See?" Bruce chuckled. "Do you think you would have *ever* landed that punch if I didn't send you to train with Scott? I made you a warrior, a competitor, you *have* to compete."

Tony leaned to the left, letting the dislocated limb hang down for a moment before rolling his shoulder back, up and around, popping it back into place. "No," he said.

"No?"

"I'm done, I'm done fighting in tournaments, I'm done fighting with you. I'm not doing it anymore," Tony spoke quietly, containing the anger in his voice and forcing Bruce to listen.

"The hell you're not! You fight in the National Open this year or else!" Bruce shouted, the vein on his shaven forehead pulsing violently in contrast with his beady blue eyes.

"No, I won't. I'm done," Tony answered.

"Then you're done here! You have ten minutes to get your shit and get out of *my* house!"

The scene shattered into a million gleaming fragments as Tony gasped for air and sat bolt upright in the plush bed. Maximus's head shot up as well, the small dog barking at an unseen threat to his master's safety.

Heck! You be go! No do scare to my hooman! The dog's child-like delivery sounded in Tony's mind, immediately easing some of the tension from the nightmare. Tony couldn't remember the last time he dreamt about being thrown out of his family home by "dear ol' dad" and would be happy to never do so again.

He pulled Maximus into a tight hug and after some initial wiggling, the pup rested his snout in the crook of his neck.

Tony lay there, holding Maximus close for a while. The dog's warmth and exhalations as he snoozed helped to push back the tidal wave of anxiety that loomed in Tony's mind.

All too soon, there was a rap on the iron door to Tony's chamber. Before he had the chance to respond the slab of metal swing open as Auren and Vasna walked in.

"Yeah, sure come on in, I'm definitely dressed and ready for company," Tony said, coating his words in sarcasm.

Auren stooped to pick up the well-worn Squire's gear and threw it onto Tony's bed. "Get ready for it then, there's work to be done," he ordered. Tony put the dozing pup down on a pillow and snatched the clothing from the comforter before exiting the safety of the bed and dressed.

Trying to fit the matching pieces along with the odd assortment of Artifact Dread Knight pieces was supremely inconvenient. The Pauldron of Vengeance leveled up, sprouting a half plate that covered the left side of his chest and back and while he could technically fit the Squire chest piece over the Pauldron, the shoulder armor had no padding.

Covenant also made it impossible for him to wear any sort of wrist or hand armor that had a left and right side, on top of that it could not be removed. He hadn't noticed it when he lay down and thinking about it now, the metal vambrace didn't feel like it was there. He rapped his knuckle against it and raised his eyebrow at the metallic *clank* that sounded.

Tony double-checked his gear and satisfied that everything was as properly equipped as it could be, looked back to the interlopers in his chamber. Auren's gaze was far off, presumably interacting with system messages from the Flagship and Vasna seemed to be inspecting him.

No longer fresh from the respawn table it was evident just how different the woman was from the other Ashtar that Tony had seen. Vasna's aspects were all over the place, her crystalline dreadlocks shone with gradients of blue and red while the strands tied off from them were a leafy green with vine-like texture.

Beyond that her eyes alternated between the piercing blue he'd seen and deep violet, the skin over her knuckles, elbows, and knees were craggy, like a cliff face while the more vulnerable areas were hardened and crystalline.

Auren piped up, "If the two of you are done eye-fucking each other we can get to work."

Tony scowled. "And what, oh mighty one, great task have you beset upon us," he asked flatly.

"Do not patronize me," Auren warned, the snap-hiss of his Battle Aura activating filling the chamber.

Tony held out his hand and the sound of a buzz saw grinding through steel drowned out the inferno for the moment it took for his Dreadblade to carve through the floor and spring into his hand. The weapon let out a metallic whine, like the toll of a bell struck with a clapper too small and dense for it. He leveled the gleaming point of the weapon at the God. "Don't threaten me," he answered.

"You don't want any of what I've got," Auren menaced, pushing his Aura outward and filling the room with it.

Tony grit his teeth, readying himself for the fight unfolding in front of him.

Rain poured from the ceiling, muting the oppressive aura. Tony looked up, confused, and when he looked down Vasna's craggy fist slammed into his face.

"What the-"

"Stop it! Both of you!" the shaman shouted. "You're both acting like asshats." Tony rubbed his jaw, and as he noticed the Battle Aura dissipating, sheathed his sword. Vasna glared into his eyes. "You good?"

"I'm fine," Tony growled.

Auren broke the settling silence. "What the hell happened to you?" the God accused.

"What do you mean?"

"You went up three levels since you left and your attributes didn't scale the way they were supposed to," he answered.

"According to the system, I Ascended. That was only after Ignacious buffed the jealous ex-fiancé of the spider-woman, who is also a princess, who I was in a ritual duel against because she and I are engaged? I think?" Tony answered. Hearing the answer out loud made Tony question the reality of it all. Was that really how it all happened?

When Tony looked back at Auren and Vasna he saw a mix of shock and disbelief across both of their faces. "What?"

"Engaged to a princess, dueling her ex, and the King of the Gods took enough notice to interfere? Seems like a little much to get done in a day." Auren said with a wry smirk.

Tony just shrugged. "I don't know what to tell you, that's how it all happened. She's in one of the regeneration pods right now. Is there a way to get some sort of notification when she's all healed up?"

It was Vasna's turn to question Tony. "What did you do to her?"

"I didn't do anything to her, her ex did after Ignacious buffed him." The Dread Knight's irritation at the barrage of questions grew by the second. "What did the two of you come in here for anyway?"

"I've been made aware that a dungeon has been generated on the Flagship. Somehow, the dungeon scaled to the highest-level Ascendants registered, which at the time were you, Vasna, and Tolik," Auren said.

"Oookay?" Tony made circles with his right hand, attempting to draw more information out of the God with the gesture.

"Dungeons, if they grow in power, can contest and invade territories, since this one's level is higher than the average level of the Ascendants onboard it's already contesting the lower levels of the Flagship. I need the two of you to go in there and clear the boss."

You have been offered a new quest!
Dungeon Delving: Clear the rogue dungeon on the Haght'anak, saving the lower-leveled Ascendants, again.
Rewards: XP, Vasna Social Link Increase, Auren Social Link Increase, Dread Knight Set Piece
Accept?
Yes   No

Tony accepted the quest, dismissing the screen that had popped up.

Auren clapped his hands. "Excellent, now we just need to find it."

"Find what?" Tony asked.

"The Dungeon."

Chapter XXI: Secret Tunnel

Tony, Vasna, Maximus, and Auren walked to the hangar. The place was a mess, equipment scattered across the former fighting pits, craters, and bits of a structure made up a majority of the debris. Tony went to scavenge the wreckage when Auren grabbed the back of his shirt.

"What?" Tony snapped, wrenching Auren's hand away.

"If you're looking for upgrades, we can go to the armory, anything you find here will not be worth it," Auren explained. His voice carried a curt edge to it.

"He's right," Vasna chipped in. "This is where Tolik ported in so most of the gear here is broken, or the durability is so low anything that might be worth it will break before you get anything out of it."

Tony looked down at Maximus. The little dog pulled his nose out of a discarded boot and looked up at Tony, wagging his tail.

"Yeah, okay. Is there familiar gear in the armory?" Maximus barked in excitement at that and leaned against Tony's leg, his tail thumping against Tony's calf.

I can has armurrs and stik for hit bad guys? Tony couldn't help but smile. He gave the dog a small nod.

"There should be," Vasna answered before Auren had the chance. "It's this way," she said as she took a left out of the hangar. The three of them followed in silence, an awkward tension hanging in the air interrupted only by the occasional bark by the small dog when someone approached too quickly.

It didn't take long for the group to arrive at the Armory, the damage caused by Tolik's assault becoming less present the further into the ship they traveled. The doors hissed open; Tony and Maximus immediately went to the side-arms section while Auren waited by the door and Vasna flipped idly through the weapon racks.

Fifteen excruciating minutes of silence passed before a word was uttered. Tony didn't mind.

There were a lot of options for him in the Armory; as a Dread Knight, he could wear Light to Heavy Armors with minimal penalties to his movement and talents he could take later would allow him to do the same with Super Heavy Armors. What he saw on the racks ranged from Leathers to Full Plate and while the idea of the ground shaking with his every step appealed to Tony, he preferred to maintain at least some mobility in battle.

He flipped back and forth between the scale mail and lamellar sets when something caught his eye behind the rack.

Tony forced the armor aside to get a good look and saw a lever sticking out of the floor; he reached for it but the weight of the armor and bulk of his arms kept the lever inches out of his reach.

Before he could think to ask, Maximus wiggled his way underneath the armor rack, gripped the lever in his teeth, and pulled.

His paws slid on the smooth metal floor for a few seconds before the pup plopped his rump on the floor and flopped onto his back, using his whole body to flip the lever.

Tony burst out laughing and fell to the floor, shattering the uncomfortable quiet in the room. Auren cracked next when he saw Maximus wiggle upright and pounce on Tony's chest, nipping playfully at the Dread Knight's chin. The God doubled over laughing and clutching his sides.

Vasna did her best to remain stoic and perused the shelves labeled "Two-Handed Blunt Weapons," but was helpless to resist when Maximus started circling Tony, half-sneezing-half-growling, before toddling toward him and swinging his tail, and therefore his rump, into Tony like a flail. Vasna kept it to a muted giggle until Maximus's tail clotheslined Tony and knocked him onto his back, then she lost it.

Tony wiped the tears from his face, some from laughing too hard, and took some steadying breaths. Maximus looked up at him, tail whipping back and forth, with a satisfied smile that only a dog can pull off.

"You rascal, you did that on purpose!" Tony said, pointing an overly accusatory finger at the small dog.

Maximus responded by tilting his head to one side and wagging his tail in short bursts.

"Dogs can always tell," Auren said.

The weight of the last few hours alleviated, Tony got to his feet and ruffled the dog's ears.

"Vasna, help me with this?" Tony asked. She obliged with a wave of her hand and gripped one end of the armor rack. "On the count of three?"

"One…Two…Three!" Vasna counted.

The metal base of the rack ground against the polished metal floor leaving deep gouges in its wake. Behind it was a tunnel that was wide enough for two people to walk side by side comfortably and tall enough that no one would need to duck or stoop to pass.

"Looks like a Dungeon Entrance to me," Tony declared. "So what do we think, secret lab with experimental weapons, secret horror factory, or someone's top-secret stash of enchanted weapons?"

"Why not all of it?" Vasna answered.

"That sounds good to me," Tony said as he strode forward. A system-generated message blared in his head:

WARNING! You are about to enter a Dungeon and are not a member of a Party. Form a Party or Dungeon Group to Proceed

Before Tony could open his mouth to ask how to form a party, a notification popped up in his vision.

Vasna has invited you to a Dungeon Group
Accept?
Yes   No

He selected "Yes" and went to step into the dungeon only to be stopped again, this time by Vasna grabbing him by the bicep and yanking him back. Tony rounded on her, but before he could say anything, she pushed some of his shredded chest armor aside, exposing the skin below.

"Forgetting something? Like, what you came here for in the first place?"

A flush rose in Tony's cheeks. She was right. The durability of his armor had been in the single digits since his fight with Tolik, let alone since bridging the Essence Circuit that revived Vasna.

He crunched some numbers and made his choices. Tony took a hardened leather cuirass, a chain shirt, iron greaves, a pair of leather dueling gloves, plate boots, and a leather belt with a brass buckle.

His armor was a mess, but given the options, he had the best blend of overall defense and maneuverability.

Helmet: The Doomed King's Helm | +10 Defense Rating

Neck: Gjöll Stone Amulet | +? Defense Rating

Chest: Hardened Leather Cuirass + Chain | +25 Defense Rating

Shoulders: Pauldron of Vengeance | +20 Defense Rating

Wrist: Covenant | +5 Defense Rating

Rings: Empty

Hands: Leather Dueling Gloves | +3 Defense Rating

Waist: Brass Buckled Leather Belt | +3 Defense Rating

Legs: Iron Greaves | +10 Defense Rating

Feet: Plate Boots | +9 Defense Rating

Tony also managed to find some armor that would fit Maximus. He outfitted the dog in a padded leather coat and a helmet that flipped down when combat started. The small dog shuffled a bit at first, but before long, he was bounding around as easily as he had been with just a collar.

I am armurred pup! Be scare of my floofy ben-gence!

It was finally time to enter the Dungeon.

Chapter XXII: Accept and Reciprocate

The vibe changed from "Space Opera desolated flagship" to "Bowels of a dying space hulk" faster than Tony cared for. Tubing and pipes hung from the walls and ceilings like entrails from an eviscerated behemoth, liquid essence pooled like blood, and cast warped shadows onto the walls. Maximus took position between Tony's legs, moving with him seamlessly with his tail tucked between his legs.

As the three of them navigated the cramped corridors, Tony took some time to examine the party screen.

Dungeon Group
Antonious King   Level: 15 Blademaster Dread Knight (Human Ascendant)   Familiar: Maximus   Level: 6* Warrior
Vasna   Level: 15 Specialized Shaman (Ascendant)

The silence was eerie and unsettling, so Tony decided to break it. "Why can't I see your Class specialization or Race in the party screen?" The question had been gnawing at him since he found the menu.

The sudden question made Vasna jump. "I have defaults set to share limited information," she explained matter-of-factly, regaining her composure.

"Ah gotcha, makes sense," he replied.

"We should probably share character screens so we can plan out how we're going to tackle this dungeon," Vasna said.

Tony nodded in agreement, glad that she had volunteered the idea, and a screen popped open in his vision.

Vasna would like to share her character screen with you (Limited)
Would you like to accept and reciprocate?
Yes   No

Accept and reciprocate? That's interesting.

Tony accepted the prompt and was notified that his character sheet would be sent over with his age, artifacts, and backgrounds concealed. He felt his eyebrow meet his hairline.

Vasna Frey	Level: 15 World Shaper Shaman (Human Ascendant)

Was the system glitching? The woman standing in front of Tony, with her varied elemental aspects, a clear indication of being Ashtar, was human?

"Dammit!" Vasna exclaimed. Tony's other eyebrow joined the former. "You gave me your Saga Debuff by sharing your sheet with me. I hope there aren't any other minions here."

Tony groaned. "You know that now there are, right? Now that you said that?" Tony replied sarcastically. How was he supposed to know that sharing information would result in sharing the "Chance for final death" debuff too?

"Whatever," Vasna said. "What else don't you know about the interface? If you didn't know how to make a party or Dungeon Group, you're probably missing a bunch of other info too."

"And you're so inclined to share now because?"

"Because now that I'm in this 'Saga' you're stuck with me until it's over. Dying sucks and now that it could be permanent, I'm not leaving until that chance goes away."

"I guess that's fair. To be honest, I don't know what I don't know. I was just kinda dumped into this and took off running."

Tony scratched the back of his head as he ducked under an impressively tangled mess of wires. "I know that my Skills and Attributes level on their own and I get points to put into them. It seems like every five levels I get a bunch of extra points too. Most of my talents seem to be prerequisite-based and pretty linear."

A flush rose in Tony's cheeks as he realized he was rambling.

"It looks like you're mostly right," Vasna offered, a far-off look in her eyes. She was reviewing information somewhere that Tony didn't have access to.

"Since you're a Dread Knight, you're on a High Attribute, Moderate Talent, Low Skill progression. I can't see your whole talent tree, but with your damage vamp talents and the damage negation from your artifacts, I should be able to keep you alive easy enough."

Most of what Vasna said surprised Tony. How did she know more about his class and progression than he did? What information did she have that he didn't?

"If you focus on, well, pretty much anything on your character screen and think 'detail,' or 'more info,' or 'I am a slab of meat with a pointy thing, teach me please,' the system will show you more information based on your Intelligence score." Vasna turned her back on him and continued walking as she continued, "Not much of a surprise that you didn't know that with your ten in Intelligence, but, it is what it is."

The insults registered but took Tony by surprise. His lowest Attribute was Luck at fifteen, why did she say his Intelligence was ten?

Accept and Reciprocate, huh, he thought. *Reciprocate must have meant sending my sheet over with the same restrictions she set on hers.*

Tony gripped the woman by the shoulder and spun her around, ducking under the massive log she swung at him and pressed her against the wall. She struggled against him, thrumming with elemental might.

Tony thought, *Send full sheet*, at the woman and her eyes went wide.

"Look, call me stupid all you want, but if that's how it's going to be, you can do whatever you need to do by yourself and I'll dismiss the Dungeon Group right now."

"I said I wasn't-" she started.

"Since you accepted my full sheet, I got yours. You and I both know that if I don't want you following me around, I can make that happen. You choose how well we get along from here."

The tension hung between them for moments that stretched into eternity. The rumbling of magic left her skin and Vasna held up her hands in a sign of surrender.

"Fine, I'm sorry I called you stupid. It's just..."

Tony raised an eyebrow and gestured for her to continue.

"You really don't have a clue, do you?" Her voice cracked.

Tony narrowed his eyes and really studied Vasna for the first time since he helped her off of the Spawning Table.

There was something familiar about her, but he couldn't place it, her body language? The half-sarcastic way she talked to him? She looked down and dug in her belt pouch for a moment before turning back to look at him when it clicked.

He remembered her standing at his door. *"Early? It's noon,"* he could hear her say.

"No way," he muttered. "You're the admin for my apartment complex?"

Her eyes widened in surprise, and a flush rose in her cheeks.

"But how did you get here?" Tony asked. There had only been three hundred "beta testers" worldwide. Two belonging to the same housing development was beyond coincidence.

"It's all your fault!" she blurted, jabbing a finger into the middle of his chest. "I went back to check on you because management noticed a power surge from your unit. The door was unlocked and when I went in you were out cold. I called the office and they sent in the med team." She shoved him, hard, and his back hit the opposite wall.

"The med team couldn't find anything wrong with you, but you were unresponsive. So they left to bring back specialists and asked me to stay. I saw the beta tester headset on the ground..." She advanced on him, fists balled by her sides and tears forming in the corners of her eyes.

"It just wasn't fair! I wanted to get into the beta too! I was active on the forums, I sent back hardware critique to Gambit, I was an active member of the community! Then you catch a lucky break to get in! Just like in-game! You have at least two artifacts and the system generates unique class pieces for you, it's not fair!"

"Look, I get it, okay. But that still doesn't explain-"

"I put on your headset. It asked me if I wanted to continue character sync, so I did. Then I was here," she admitted, barely above a whisper.

Tony's eyes widened as Vasna collapsed into his chest. "Hey," he offered, not sure what to do. Did he hug her? Take a few giant steps back before she acquainted him with the business end of her tree? Maximus nudged him forward, pressing the top of his head against the back of Tony's leg.

If this blows up in my face, I'm giving you a bath, Tony menaced.

Maximus chuffed, almost as if he could read Tony's thoughts.

Tony dismissed the notion and put his arms around Vasna. She stiffened but relented as he gently pulled her close. He felt the tears dripping onto his chest, silent at first, but the floodgates opened, and with the release of emotion came body-wracking sobs.

It was too much.

Vasna had been resolute up until just a couple of minutes ago. Maybe she had been putting on a brave face, trying to plow forward, just like Tony was. As she continued to cry, Tony felt his own resolve weaken. He was determined not to acknowledge his own hurt and despair and now, less than an hour into the dungeon, was on the brink of tears himself.

A fist slamming into his side knocked the wind out of him and completely disrupted his focus. When he looked down at Vasna, her bleary eyes met his.

"Just cry with me, dammit," she sobbed.

If Tony's emotions were jammed behind a wall, Vasna was a sledgehammer. All at once, Tony's eyes stung, his stomach flopped, and the lump in his throat that he had pressed down so many times finally breached. Maximus hopped back as Tony and Vasna both sunk to their knees, clutching to each other and sobbing.

Tony's eyes opened to Vasna cradling his head against her chest. She was humming and stroking his hair, pausing to sniffle on occasion.

Maximus was curled up in the crook of Tony's leg, and when he started to stir, the dog's curled tail wagged, slapping against Tony's thigh. The elemental signs had disappeared from her body, and with the exception of the undercut, dreadlocks, and no glasses, Vasna looked *exactly* like the admin.

"What happened?" Tony croaked, his voice hoarse.

Vasna's voice was not that of a woman who had been sobbing for an unknown amount of time, but of a caretaker. "You stopped holding yourself up and passed out. At first, I thought you were trying the 'super sad boy, love me' card because when you went out, you pulled me on top of you. Sorry about the jaw, by the way."

Tony worked his mouth for a moment, and there was indeed a shot of pain that ran through it.

"I'm sure I'll deserve that at some point," he said.

Her laugh was soft and melodic. "After that, I realized that you were actually out cold. Then you started talking, said that you were cold. This dungeon is definitely going to take both of us to clear, especially with what I saw wandering around."

Tony's eyes flicked around the hallway, searching for "what had been wandering around." He could make out his weapons and most of the armor he had come into the dungeon wearing.

When he looked down toward Maximus, he saw most of his clothes scattered on the ground.

"Uh, I'm not naked under this blanket, am I?" Tony asked, not sure if he wanted to hear the answer.

Jorogu's gonna be real mad, he thought.

Vasna's knee nudged his gut. "What kinda perv do you think I am?" she cooed indignantly. "You still have your pants on. You were shivering, what else was I supposed to do?"

"You know body heat transfers through clothes too right? The whole naked in a sleeping bag thing is a myth." Maybe if he wasn't dehydrated and exhausted the joke would have come across better.

Vasna rolled her eyes with such intensity he could feel it. "Not if I'm using my 'Warmth' spell."

Tony found his arms slung around her waist, pinned by the small of her back against the blanket wrapped around the two of them. The matter settled, Vasna began humming and stroking his hair again.

She was very warm.

Chapter XXIII: Legion

Tony, Vasna, and Maximus broke from their "cuddle puddle" after what Tony thought was about an hour. His face felt heavy and his throat was raw, however, the tremendous angst that had built in his chest and across his shoulders had been relieved. His body moved easier, his armor felt lighter, and not dragging his feet got just a little easier.

A chime, like silverware hitting the side of a giant crystal cup, sounded urgently in Tony's head, alerting him to a litany of ignored notifications.

Your Unseen Ally Background has been revealed!
Your Social Link with Vasna has increased to Level 1!
Your Social Link with Vasna has increased to Level 2!
Your Social Link with Vasna has increased to Level 3!
Your Social Link with Vasna has increased to Level 4!

Tony rolled his eyes, not at the news, but at the redundancy of the notifications.

He turned to look at Vasna as they walked down the hallway and paused, feeling like he was really seeing her for the first time.

Maybe it was knowing who she was outside of the "game" or maybe it was from being a blubbering mess in her lap just moments before, but he had to stop and look.

Her piercing blue eyes had lost a measure of their initial harshness, replaced instead with a fearsome sense of guardianship. The smooth section of her hair which had been pinned tightly against her scalp was tousled, hanging loosely along the left side of her head before coming to the relaxed tail of dreadlocks. The woman he had met on the Spawning Table would have been more than happy to acquaint him with the business end of her tree-made-mace; this woman he felt safe with.

Her eyebrow arched at his continued gaping. "Uh, sorry," Tony started, "is there a way to consolidate notifications?"

She smirked at him. "Tired of getting the same notification with a different number at the end?" Tony nodded. "You can go into settings and switch notifications to 'summary.' You can mess with it from there." she explained.

Tony took a minute and did just that; he set his level-up notifications to announce only the highest level of any trait achieved at level up and then set notifications to only play on request unless ten or more ranks in a trait had been gained. That done, he requested a summative notification for the last three hours.

Your Unseen Ally Background has been revealed!
You have gained Skill Bonuses: Resolve +2 (Current Level: 7)
You have gained the Skill: Empathy (Current Level: 3 [-2 from Clueless Flirt: Females Trait])

You are Rested (Spirit)
You are Tired (Physical)
You are Dehydrated
You are Hungry
Maximus has Unspent: Specialization, Attribute, Skill,
Talent Points
Your Dreadblade is Unnamed
Your Dreadblade has Unspent Upgrade Points
You have unlocked an Achievement: Romance or Something
More?
Spend more than an hour in the embrace of another
The Dungeon has increased in Difficulty – You'd Better
Hurry!

Tony's eyes shot wide and he could tell that Vasna had been reviewing at least some of the same information from the curses she was muttering and he would be kidding himself if he wasn't upset about forgetting to upgrade his Dreadblade.

I wonder if I can upgrade that since I'm not spending MY XP?

The breath caught in Tony's chest. His Social Link with Jorogu had only gone up to five after they had sex in the bathhouse and he'd "accepted" her marriage proposal. The Social Link with Vasna hitting four and the Achievement that came with it, what did that mean? His link with Jorogu hadn't decreased and there was no other Social notification to review.

Tony took some deep breaths and thought about his Dreadblade Screen. There was a time and place to sort out potential relationship issues, and this was neither. His weapon upgrade menu sprang open in his vision.

> Please Name your Dreadblade: |

Tony held back the initial urge to name the Dreadblade "Kindness" and mulled over some options before finding one that fit.

> You have named your Dreadblade "Legion"
>
> Confirm Name?   Yes   No

Tony focused on confirming and a new box sprang forward.

> Our number is as your will, innumerable and insurmountable. We answer the call: Vae Victis.

> You have learned the invocation for your Dreadblade!

Tony focused on the new notification and was rewarded with additional information.

> Summon Dreadblade (Invocation) – Using Summon Dreadblade with the proper invocation summons the weapon with all enhancements activated and at full charge.

Tony winced as the words "Vae Victis" were burned into his memory. When he regained his focus he was looking at the upgrade screen.

Legion: Level 5 Dreadblade

Form: Bastard Sword   Heritage: Italian (Roman) Tier: Uncommon

Bonuses: Derived   Phylactery: Advanced Summon: Dynamic

Speed: 4   Accuracy: 11   Defense: 10   Capacity: 22 Damage: 17   Discharge: 26   Range: 18

Enhancements: None   Enchantments: None

You have one Rare Enchantment Available (Soul of Tolik the Knave) You have two Uncommon Enchantments Available You have four Common Enchantments Available You have five Enhancements Available

Tony's head spun with the information but was relieved to know that enhancing his equipment was possible in a dungeon. Looking through the Enchantments, he realized that they were very similar to conventional weapon enhancements from games like Dungeons and Dragons, with the intensity dialed up to eleven. Enhancements were still powerful, but more mundane, typically modifying the physical features of the dark iron blade to enhance the weapon's base stats. Tony decided to start there.

Enhancements (Available)
Broadened Fuller
Honed Edge
Blade Balancing
Agile Handle
Aggressive Pommel
Broadened Guard
Reinforced Construction
Mutable Form
Efficient Construction
Enhanced Physics

Feeling the need to move quickly, he made the selections of Reinforced Construction, Efficient Construction, Enhanced Physics, Honed Edge, and Blade Balancing. The fact that "Reinforced Construction" existed caused Tony to think that there was the potential for his blade to be broken or sundered and while he could simply resummon it, the Dreadblade could be re-summoned in its broken state.

With that in mind, reinforcing the construction could add to the weight of the blade, and while he was sure that his considerable strength could handle the additional weight, tuning the blade to be more agile in combat without changing its makeup significantly would be a tremendous benefit.

Honed edge was a given, assuming it did what he thought, adding to the damage potential of the weapon and keeping it from being stuck in anyone unfortunate enough to be intimately introduced to the bladed part.

Tony moved onto the enchantments and thought at the system, *Give me a recommended list.*

Available Enchantments (Recommended)
Rare
Intelligent   Vorpal Dancing   Doubling
Uncommon
Dueling   Elemental Burst Raging   Spell Stealing Spectral Anchoring
Common
Returning   Elemental Bane   Defending Axiomatic   Anarchic Immaculate   Anchoring Benevolent Kinetic Momentum

Tony rolled his eyes. This being a consolidated list meant that there had to be many options that he could spend hours sifting through. He pressed down the desire to do so with his urgency. Anchoring and Elemental showing up in different variations in Common and Uncommon piqued his interest.

Elemental was straightforward enough, it would add a basic element of his choosing to his blade from Fire, Water, Earth, Air, and Wood and if he layered two compatible elements, they would make a third hybrid element.

Fire and Water would make Steam, while Fire and Air would make Lightning; as appealing as making his weapon have combination elements was, taking two enchantments to do so was less so. Elemental burst caught him by surprise. It acted almost exactly as the Elemental enchantment but scoring a decisive or overkill blow would cause an elemental detonation that the weapon would protect him from. The gears in Tony's head ground to a stop when he realized that he could blend his Common and Uncommon enchantments to create hybrid elements.

Anchoring in Common would add tremendous weight to the weapon as soon as it left Tony's hands. In theory, he could impale an enemy to a wall and walk away, requiring truly gargantuan strength to remove the weapon holding them in place.

Spectral Anchoring, on the other hand, would allow Tony to spend a set amount of Lore to leave a phantom blade instead that could not be removed until Tony released the Lore or the pinned enemy died. While he considered something like this to be a little morbid, having access to an effect like this could help greatly in fights against giant monsters or opponents that were exceptionally nimble.

After moments of painstaking internal deliberation, Tony made his decisions.

Legion: Level 5 Dreadblade (Enhanced, Enchanted)
Form: Bastard Sword Heritage: Italian (Roman) Tier: Uncommon Bonuses: Derived Phylactery: Advanced Summon: Dynamic Speed: 16 Accuracy: 19 Defense: 20 Capacity: 28 Damage: 27 (48.6 2H) Discharge: 32 Range: 24
Enhancements:
Honed Edge: 6 to speed Bonus to retrieve the weapon from mass Reinforced Construction: 2 to all weapon stats Efficient Construction: 4 to all weapon stats Blade Balancing: Increased weapon handling +2 to Accuracy and Defense Enhanced Physics: Causes knockback 1.8x DMG when two handed +4 Damage
Enchantments:

Rare (1 of 4)

Intelligent: Forms a telepathic and spiritual bond with the wielder

Uncommon (2 of 6)

Elemental Burst (Fire): Wreathes the weapon in Fire, adding elemental damage to attacks. Decisive Blows and Overkill triggers an elemental explosion

Spectral Anchoring: Spend 20 Lore to leave a phantom blade in a living target, pinning them to the spot

Common (4 of 8)

Bane (Divine): Gains bonus accuracy and damage vs (Divine) creatures and Constructs

Defending: Gains a permanent +2 Defense Bonus

Elemental (Earth): Gain bonus Elemental Damage and +30% Lightning Resist

Kinetic Momentum: Continuous hits against a single Target gain +2% Damage per successive hit, to a maximum of 120%

Focusing his intent on his Pet screen, he received an error from the system. Being inside the dungeon would not prevent him from upgrading and enhancing his weapon, but it would prevent him from upgrading his familiar until the next level-up.

Exasperated, Tony dismissed his screens and jogged to catch up with Vasna, Maximus on his heel.

Chapter XXIV: Leveled Player, Crawling Dungeon

The first groups of enemies that they encountered were not difficult to dispatch but left both Tony and Vasna shaken. The Rotten, constructs made of flesh, tubing from the ship's innards, and metal groaning pleas for final death while actively trying to kill you would have left most shaking in their boots. The only one unfazed by the encounters with the "constructs" was Maximus.

The fearless dog had jumped right into the fray when the first construct nearly gutted Tony, slamming it in the chest with his head and pinning it to the ground with his front paws. Maximus had torn the thing's head clear off with his teeth clamped around its neck. Then he padded over and dropped it at Tony's feet, his curly tail wagging like a helicopter propeller. After that, the pair of Ascendants handily dispatched the occasional swarms of the Rotten.

Tony wasn't sure if it was simply due to the enhancements made to his weapon or due to the light frames of his enemies.

Still, with each second or third swing of his newly improved Dreadblade, they shattered into messy pieces and soared from him, slamming into and sometimes through the walls of the corridor.

He chalked the lack of enchantments up to needing to resummon his Dreadblade or to call its Invocation. The gamer in him wanted to swing around his newly enchanted and powered-up weapon of doom, but an eerie sensation of being watched told him that he should wait. Tony had learned to listen to those feelings.

Maximus was level six, according to the Companion Sub-Menu, and Tony couldn't help but wonder if he was level capped due to unspent trait points. Thinking back on it, Maximus had been level 5 when he found him, there was no way that he hadn't gained enough XP to level more than once in the time they had been together.

Tony cursed inwardly. They'd moved so rapidly from one thing to the next that he had barely spent his own trait points and specializations. He hadn't even touched Maximus's.

With this realization came an all-too-familiar sense of regret. The Maximus he knew in his old life had died suddenly; tumors had formed around his bladder and his heart. The decision to lay him to rest had to be made quickly.

The doctor told him that they could have given him maybe a couple more days, but the tumors were too close to vital organs to remove and another day would have been a blessing.

The chance that Maximus could have collapsed due to the pressure put on his heart as soon as an hour after they left the animal hospital made Tony feel that trying for the extra time would have been selfish.

Tony had struggled internally for months after that, wondering if he had been a bad "dog dad." In hindsight, the accidents inside and sluggishness were glaring signs that something was wrong. But in the moment, Tony had only gotten frustrated with the ailing dog.

He hated himself for that. He had a hard time breathing past the lump forming in his throat when he felt Vasna's hand rest on his exposed skin, just above the bracer on his right arm. Tony nearly jumped at the contact.

"What's going on up there?" she asked, her eyes boring into the side of Tony's head.

He set his jaw and pushed those feelings down, now wasn't the time.

> **Vasna didn't like that.**

The notification popped up right as Vasna's fist slammed into the side of his face, catching him entirely off-balance and sending him careening into a mess of tubes and metal. "Stop that!" she yelled. Tony looked back at her, confused.

"Stop what?" he grunted, flexing against the tubes and wires.

"Repressing your emotions!" she yelled.

Tony's eyes flicked to his status bars; there was no debuff there to represent his stifled feelings.

Vasna rolled her eyes. "I don't need to see a debuff to see that look you make when you think about something sad and then clench your jaw to force it down. My Empathy skill is at ten, you're not hiding anything like that from me." Tony tore himself free from the guts of the wall.

"Can we talk about this later?" Tony's mouth formed a hard line.

"No, we're talking-"

"I mean after we deal with that," he cut her off, pointing down the hall over her shoulder.

Vasna whirled. A behemoth of wires, metal, tubing, incandescent liquid essence, and flesh lumbered toward them.

The thing's bulk was immense, forcing the hall's walls out. More liquid essence poured from the gaping wounds in the ceiling and over the beast, illuminating its myriad faces. Their rictus maws split open in unison and loosed a terrible roar that boomed through the confined space.

"Cover me!" Vasna shouted as she slung her tree-trunk-made-mace over her shoulder and clapped her hands together. The sound reverberated through the hall, chasing the echoes of the roar from the space.

Tony looked at Maximus then back to the monster. "I promise to spend your points when we're out of here, boy. I need you to stay back and protect her, alright?" Maximus barked an affirmative and stood in front of Vasna, hackles raised and teeth bared.

I got dis!

Tony drew Legion and took off at a sprint as Vasna began to chant.

"Great Spirit of the East, Great-grandfather fire, Spirit of the new day, Eternal fire of the sun, hear my plea. From you comes our life energy, vital spark, the power to see greatness, to envision with boldness. You who purify the senses, our hearts, and our minds. We humbly ask that we may be aligned with you, that your energy may flow through us, and be expressed by us for the good of this realm and all living things upon it." As she spoke, her voice grew in volume, smoke poured from her skin, and sparks erupted from the slightest friction. At the end of the passage, an aura of fire erupted from her.

Vasna turned to the South.

Tony was under siege before he reached the horrid amalgam, tendrils coated in essence and tipped with jagged scraps of metal and bone lashed out at him as the beast lumbered toward him. The Dread Knight weaved side to side, narrowly dodging the strikes.

I have to stop it before it gains too much momentum! he thought and activated Battle Rush.

The burst of speed hurtled Tony into engagement range, and the Doomed King's Helm slammed into place just in time to deflect a razor-tipped attack.

Legion's edge slammed into the monstrosity, arresting its momentum, and the muscles in Tony's shoulders and back screamed with effort as the thing pushed against him.

Vasna's prayer continued.

"Great Spirit of the South, protector of the lands and of all things growing, the noble trees and grasses. Great-grandmother earth, Guardian Spirit of nature, power of receptiveness, of nurturance and endurance, bringing forth the flowers of the fields, fruits of the orchards, and of the garden. We humbly ask that we may be aligned with you, that your power may flow through us for the good of this earth and all living things upon it." The metal of the halls groaned as vines and flowering bushes grew out of them, reaching for Vasna. The fire surrounding her did not scorch the plants, but caressed them, spurring their growth.

Vasna turned to the West.

Tony weaved between the behemoth's bulldozer-like "hands" and fended off a flurry of blows from the sinuous tubing that hung from seemingly everywhere on the beast. He had gotten the thing to stop but had no idea what Vasna was doing, or what would happen if the glowing green essence dripped on his skin. Legion was seemingly unaffected as Tony carved through the softer surfaces of the monster with his parries.

Tony heard Maximus bark and then the sound of something slamming into a wall behind him. A cold sweat broke out across his back, and he looked.

Maximus was barking at one of the smaller scrap flesh amalgams that he had seemingly headbutted into the wall.

Tony barely managed to pull Legion up in front of him as his moment of terror cost him thirty percent of his HP bar; twenty percent from the thing's car-sized fist slamming into him, and another ten percent from slamming into the far wall. Tony tasted copper and pulled himself free of the crumpled metal wall.

The beast was moving to walk past him.

"Where do you think you're going?" he grunted, spitting blood onto the floor. "I'm not done with you!"

"Great spirit of the West, Spirit of the great waters of rivers, lakes, springs, and rains. Great-grandmother ocean, the deepest matriarch, the womb of all life. With you comes the dissolving of boundaries and of limitations, the power to taste, feel, cleanse, and heal. Great blissful darkness of peace. We humbly ask that we may be aligned with you, that your power may flow through us, for the good of this realm and all living things upon it." Vasna's skin rippled and glowed a translucent blue, shining like Earth's sky reflected in a lake of crystal.

Vasna turned to face North.

Challenging the beast to face him again accomplished a few things at once. The beast roared, and hundreds of tendrils lashed out at Tony at once. Some cut him as they grabbed at him hungrily, costing him another ten percent of his HP. It was impossible to dodge and cut through all of the appendages surging at him. Tony was wrapped up in vitriol-coated tubes before he could escape the area-of-effect grapple attack.

Just before his vision was completely cut off, he looked back to Maximus. The dog's eyes were conflicted. Tony had told him to guard Vasna and the lesser amalgams continued to approach her at a snail's pace.

If she weren't stuck channeling she would be more than fine, but that wasn't the case. The tendrils blacked out Tony's vision and all he could see was his remaining HP ticking down at one percent per second. Maximus let out a low mournful howl.

Tony's mind flashed back to the argument he'd had with his father. *"You didn't deserve that mutt, you didn't take care of him. This is what you get!"* He wouldn't subject Maximus to the same sorrow he experienced.

Tony activated Invincible Will and The Pauldron of Vengeance activated with it, putting his Lore bar to fifty percent.

Tony pushed out with every ounce of strength he could muster. He felt tubing snap and metal creak and break away from him.

It wasn't enough.

Tony dumped another ten percent of his Lore into the Invincible Will Talent for the upgrade effect, increasing his strength by twenty percent. He tossed out any notion of restraint and roared with effort, rage, and sorrow.

He wasn't done, Maximus needed him, Vasna needed him, *Jorogu* needed him.

Vasna turned sharply to the North. Urgency pumped the final passage of the chant out, and her Talent activated forming four gargantuan pillars. The totems formed from glass that contained a lightning storm, obsidian with streaks of glowing magma running through its vibrant coral surface, its core pulsing with bio-luminescent light, and perfect spheres of Iron, Aluminum, and Copper orbited around an orb of pulsing viridian light.

Greater Invocation of Wind Totem – Haste increased by thirty-five percent.
Greater Invocation of Flame Totem – Damage increased by forty percent, Regeneration increased by twenty percent.
Greater Invocation of Water Totem – Damage taken reduced by twenty percent.
Greater Invocation of Earth Totem – Armor increased by fifty percent.

The four totems, more like monoliths in size, pulsed once more, applying the buffs to Tony and Maximus before they condensed to orbit around Vasna's head.

Greater Crown of Elemental Invocation – in addition to the effects of Greater Invocation Totems, all elemental damage dealt by the Shaman is increased by one hundred percent, all healing effects are applied twice, any Elementals summoned by the Shaman are increased by one category.

Vasna was ready.

A wave of energy hit Tony as soon as he was mostly freed from the biomechanical cage that gave him the last of what he needed to liberate himself entirely. As his feet met the ground, Maximus soared past him, a glowing, snarling mass of auburn fur, and slammed into the behemoth. Liquid essence, scraps of metal, tubing, and chunks of necrotized flesh flew from the hole that the enhanced Maximus carved through the beast.

The behemoth recoiled and wailed. Vasna streaked past Tony next, her fists wreathed in blazing stone and fire.

I always wanted to try this! he heard her speak into his mind.

"Shoryuken!" she shouted, leaping into the air to deliver a crushing uppercut into the "primary chin" of the monster, nearly tipping it into its back. The flame on her fists detonated on impact and cleaved off half of the thing's faces.

Tony dumped the remainder of his Lore points into three successive Adamant Slashes, the indigo waves slashed through the behemoth's arms at the shoulders and vaporized its remaining visage. Maximus bounded free of the collapsing corpse before it dissolved into essence slush and seeped through the floor.

Achievement Unlocked: Miniboss Slayer! - You have slain your First Dungeon Miniboss. Gratz!

Despite the joyous tone of the notification, Tony's shoulders slumped. "That was the Miniboss?"

Vasna approached him. "I wouldn't worry about that too much, you soloed the thing for the most part, and my Greater Invocation will be active for the rest of the Dungeon."

Encounter Experience Gained!

Ship Guts Flesh Amalgam x 50

Experiment 12 (Fetid Survivor Golem) x 1

The experience will be divided among your Active Group

Level Up!

Congratulations, you have reached Level 16!

Legion Absorbed the Soul Construct of Experiment 12!

Legion will require [12 hours] to Process Enchantments and Enhancements

You have [30 Minutes] to spend Points

Your Core Attributes have Increased!

You have 4 Attribute Points Available

You have 5 Skill Points Available

You have 2 Talent Points available

Invincible Will+ is ready to be Upgraded

Oath is ready to be Upgraded

Adamant Slash is ready to be Upgraded

Things had gotten dire during the fight with "Experiment 12," but Vasna's buffs had come through in a huge way. With time ticking away, he jumped directly into Maximus's Character Sheet.

What he saw was not surprising, Maximus's stats were average for a Familiar, though his Charisma was exceptionally high.

Tony looked to Maximus for approval with every point and talent selection made. The little dog would either pant and wag his tail, meaning yes, or sneeze and shake his head for no.

Maximus: Level 11 Canis Familiaris
Class: Warrior (5) | Dire Hound (5) | Dog of War (1)

Attributes
Strength 18   Dexterity 15   Endurance 18 Charisma 22   Wisdom 8   Spirit 10 Intelligence 10   Wits 16   Luck 10

Skills
Brawl 10   Awareness 15   Survival 8 Fortitude 5   Athletics 5   Tandem Tactics 10

Talents
Spirit Pet Weapon Training (Martial)   Armor Training (Light) Intoned Call   Empath   Crushing Bite   Maul Awareness   Evasive   Alert   Instinct Signal

As soon as Tony confirmed the changes to Maximus's sheet, the dog changed rapidly. His fur took on a lamellar-like sheen, his nails hardened and sharpened to rending claws, and his puppy-friendly armor split and tore off of him as he nearly quadrupled in size.

The maybe twelve-pound pup that had yipped and flopped around was now almost two hundred pounds of battle hound who could look Tony in the eyes. Maximus stared at Tony, seeming confused to be so tall before his tail started to wag and he assaulted Tony's face with unrelenting kisses.

"Ack! Max! Gimme a minute, I need to spend my points too you know!" The Maximus back on Earth would have paused for maybe half a second, and then continued anyway, but this one understood the urgency in Tony's voice, at the very least, and sat to wait. He was only a head shorter than Tony sitting. Tony went for his upgrades first. Invincible Will + upgraded to

Indomitable Self - In addition to the effects of Invincible Will +, upon activation, the Dread Knight gains 100% of their Maximum HP as Temporary Hit Points and is immune to Crowd Control Effects until those Hit Points are lost. Lore Capacity is permanently increased by 15%

Pleased with the permanent addition of Lore, Tony noticed a trend that quickened his pulse.

The initial upgrade to Invincible Will had come in handy, but wasn't anything "game-breaking," but its seemingly final upgrade to Indomitable Self was truly awesome. What had easily become Tony's favorite Talent, Adamant Slash, upgraded to

Adamant Slash + - When using Adamant Slash the Dread Knight may spend an additional 5% Lore to add the following effects
Splitting Beam - Two lesser waves split from the initial attack, seeking the nearest enemy targets after impacting with an enemy.
Adamant Blade - Instead of projecting the attack, [Adamant Blade] contains the Lore to discharge and instead increases the damage and physics of the next attack made by the Dread Knight.
Overcharge (Stackable) - For every 2 applications of [Overcharge] the effects of Adamant Slash are doubled. [Overcharge] precludes the use of other Adamant Slash + effects.

Tony let out a low whistle.

Now THAT's an upgrade! he thought. He hadn't activated Oath since his "showdown" with Ignacious, but he had to guess that being under the effects of the Oath that he made to avenge D had been what made it eligible for an upgrade.

Sacred Vow - An Oath sworn on the Dread Knight's very soul. When a Dread Knight invokes a Sacred Vow, no power can sway them from it. All attempts to dissuade a Dread Knight from fulfilling their Vow automatically fail. Another perfect effect will be contested by the Dread Knight, and they receive their (Essence + Spirit Modifier) as a bonus to resist. Should the Dread Knight fail to complete the terms of their Vow, the Archon will come to collect.

Using his two Talent Points, Tony picked up Asphyxiate and Runeforging.

Asphyxiate		
Cost: 15 Lore	Duration: Instant	Damage: None
Effect: The Dread Knight crushes the Magic within his foes by sheer force of will. Talents or spells that have vocal components are interrupted. Spells or talents from the same discipline are silenced for ten seconds.		

Against a Mage-class enemy, ten seconds with no magic being slung his way could turn the tables very quickly.

Runeforging	
Cost: Varies	Duration: Varies
Effect: Inscribe Runes into non-artifact arms and armor increasing their effectiveness and granting bonus effects. Lore cost and Inscription time is dependent on the rune inscribed	

Runeforging seemed more like a profession skill than a talent, but if he could put his mundane armor pieces on a similar level to his Artifact pieces, it would be well worth it.

Your Party has been challenged by the Dungeon Boss!

Go forward and conquer!

Chapter XXV: Boss Fight

Character Sheet
Name: Antonious King   Race: Ascendant   Essence: 4 Class: Squire (5) | Knight (5) | Dread Knight [Blademaster] (6)
Attributes Strength: 30   Charisma: 20   Intelligence: 20 Dexterity: 22   Wisdom: 21   Wits: 21 Endurance: 30   Spirit: 30   Luck: 15
Skills Melee – 20   Awareness – 10   Occult – 10 Survival – 5   Fortitude – 16   Athletics (Freerunning) – 10 Socialize - 5   Tandem Tactics: (5)   Resolve: 6   Empathy: 5
Sagas: Active Saga: War Against Heaven Backgrounds: Artifact: Pauldron of Vengeance   Covenant Gjöll Stone Amulet Familiar: Maximus
Talents Summon Dreadblade (Life-Biting Essence) Berserker's Stance   Frenzied Blood Rapture Pommel Strike   Punishing Parry Oath   Sacred Vow Knight's Charge   Battle Rush   Asphyxiate Invincible Will+   Indomitable Self   Runeforging Fatal Resolve   Adamant Slash+   Bloody Haste

Contrary to what happened when Jorogu challenged Tony, the party being challenged teleported the group straight into the boss chamber. The room was expansive and circular, glass panels illuminated the chamber and its contents, the lab of a madman.

"You did well to reach me here," a voice echoed over the loudspeaker, "and to have destroyed my latest creation. You know what they say though, thirteen is a lucky number."

"Let me guess, this is the part where you monologue us to death?" Tony interrupted. He knew these fights well enough, confront the evil genius in his lab, he monologues, sends his minions out in waves to survive through, then when you fight the boss your resources and cooldowns are spent just dealing with the mobs so you have to fight at lessened capacity.

"Not at all, Ascendant. It would be where I analyze the subjects for my next experiment. The three of you and maybe even the Daimyo Arach in the regeneration pod upstairs will make for a sufficient amalgam to end this pathetic project," the voice said.

A chill ran up Tony's spine that was swiftly burned away by anger. "Now I know you didn't just threaten my dog-"

"Oh? Going to get angry now, are you? Well, I've prepared for that."

Shit, Tony thought, *was that why I felt like I was being watched on the ship?*

A set of bay doors on the ground hissed open and dumped a horde of the Rotten constructs into the room and snapped closed. Tony looked to Vasna. "Do you want me to take them, or do you want them?"

The shaman just shrugged. "I'll take those, you take that group and the dog takes the rest?" she offered up.

Without another word the three of them jumped into action; blade, claws, fangs, and Vasna's mace flashed through the mob of Rotten with ease and precision. Fifty of the constructs went down in just under ninety seconds.

"That's impressive, even for a pair of Ascendants. Your performance beats the last record by fourteen point three seconds. Experiment thirteen will certainly be impressive," the voice said.

"You want us for your experiment, come and claim us yourself, lazy ass!" Vasna shouted.

Tony smirked. "Do you think he'd really-"

"As you wish," the voice answered.

An instant later the whir of a hydraulic lift echoed through the chamber. "Well son of a bitch," Tony muttered.

A section of the wall opened up and a man emerged; more than half of his body was either made of metal or had metal grafted to it. His left eye was an insidious red orb in the silhouette standing in the lift.

Mendacius	Level: 20 Dungeon Boss (Divine)
Heart of the Infernal Machine	

He spread his arms and walked into the room. "Still content to call me lazy? Allow me to show you the results of my hard work!" With that, the whole room came alive. Images of bladed machines, fire, and death across the cosmos. "You see-"

Tony interrupted the machine-man's monologue with a combo of Battle Rush and Adamant Slash stacked with Adamant Blade. The attack caught Mendacius flat-footed and pushed him back, the metal of Tony's charged Dreadblade sparking against the Boss's mechanical arms.

Mendacius's chest parted and crackling red essence gathered over the center. Tony attempted to break engagement but metal fingers wrapped around and plunged into his forearms, claiming ten percent of his HP. "Don't worry, Antonious, this won't kill you. I need you to tell me how this feels."

Heck you, buzz man! Maximus's voice sounded in his head. The dog charged forward and clamped his maw around one of Mendacius's legs.

It must have been one of his organic legs since the man growled in pain. He kicked the dog across the room.

Vasna soared over Maximus, giant log-made-mace held overhead, a metal tube popped out of Mendacius's shoulder and discharged the same red essence. The blast washed over the woman and forced her back.

"I'm gonna kill you!" Tony roared.

"Now, Antonious, do tell me how much this hurts." The metal-man's attack went off, claiming fifty percent of Tony's HP. The upside to taking such a severe amount of damage was that it freed the Dread Knight from the Dungeon Boss's metal grip. Tony slammed the tip of Legion into the floor to arrest his momentum; a deep furrow followed him to where he landed.

Use me, the voice from Arach bellowed in his mind, *use me and win!* The Dreadblade let out the same high-pitched toll it did when it came out of the floor. Tony grit his teeth.

"Vae Victis." With the Invocation came a rush of power and a high-pitched whine that shattered the glass screens and shook the room. Mendacius roared in pain. Tony looked over and saw him clutching his head; now was his chance.

He rushed forward and slashed at both of his legs and chest, spending twenty Lore each time and nearly bottoming out his pool to pin the Boss's legs in place and the plates concealing the cannon in his chest shut.

Vasna's tree trunk soared from the back end of the room, magma, lightning, and frost trailing from the business end. It collided with the metal-man's chest and caved in the plating, rending it inoperable. Tony glimpsed back at her and saw her cast a chain heal on Maximus that transferred over to him.

The dog was scrabbling to his feet, unable to find purchase on the metal floor, but seemed fine otherwise.

The walls of the room began to split open; tendrils of wire coated with the same vitriolic essence and blades thrashed from the wounds. Mendacius limped toward the lift.

"Looks like we flipped the boss phases," Tony shouted over the din. "Do you have an AOE that can clear these?" Vasna just grinned in answer.

Her elemental aspects flared back to the surface and all reconfigured. Where vines had been, hair streams of lightning replaced them, her eyes surged with electricity, and portions of her body became ethereal storm clouds.

Bolt after bolt of levin fury pounded the room, driving back the writhing death coming from the walls and sealing off Mendacius's escape.

Tony paid the ten percent HP cost to activate Bloody Haste and surged after the boss.

He turned and pointed one of his sizzling arm cannons at Tony, as the essence built up, Tony activated his Asphyxiate talent and the glow guttered out.

The awakened Legion held in both hands, Tony flexed every ounce of power he could muster and pressed the assault. Chunks of metal flew away first as Mendacius attempted to deflect the attacks with his artificial limbs; after the Dread Knight carved through those, he swung again and again.

Maximus let out a loud bark that broke Tony from his fugue long enough for Vasna to get between him and the remnants of a torso atop a single leg.

"It's okay, you got him, we're all okay." Her hands ran over his blood-covered face and hair and Legion clattered to the floor.

Tony sunk to his knees, the exertion of the fight catching up with him all at once. Vasna cradled his head against her chest.

"We're all okay, Max is good, he was fine before I even cast the heal, I promise," she continued.

The war dog padded up to the two of them and sniffed into Tony's ear.

Okay Daddy? I okay, you okay? Tony smiled as the dog licked the tears and blood from his face.

"I got so scared," he admitted, "that if he hurt you..." he trailed off.

Logically, he knew that the Maximus here was far more resilient than the pet he had loved, that if this Maximus fell, he had the item needed to revive him. That didn't stop his emotions from flaring, from the need to make up for what he thought he had done wrong bludgeoning his conscience.

One of Vasna's hands cupped the side of his face and pulled it up to meet her gaze.

The soft look in her eyes, her slightly lifted chin and parted lips registered too late for Tony to say anything about it.

She kissed him, hard. Her lips were cool and sizzled against his own, like a molten iron passing through a slab of ice.

One arm around her waist, the other under her butt like a seat, he scooped her up and pressed her against the first wall he found. She wrapped her legs around his torso, cementing the lip-lock.

You have unlocked an Achievement!

Dungeoneering Apprentice - Clear your first Dungeon

Chapter XXVI: The Queen Wakes

Tony woke up to Maximus's massive head flopping onto his stomach. "Oomph!" he gasped. "Buddy, you just gotta tell me you want to get up, not try to kill me geez!"

The dog breathed into Tony's face, *Daddy get up for playtime? Play pull war game?*

Tony scratched the big dog behind the ears. "Yeah we'll play in a bit, buddy, I just need to wake up and clean up, okay?"

Yayy! Maximus cheered, jumping off the bed and zooming around the room.

Things had been quiet in the days after clearing the dungeon. Tony and Vasna had gone off for a few hours to clear her familiar quest which granted her a beast familiar called a Kraul. The cub was a blend between a hyena, an elephant, and a saber-toothed tiger with the disposition of a quokka. She named the cub Embry.

Vasna had stayed in Tony's room the night after the dungeon. He was in an awkward position. Jorogu was still in the regeneration pod, or he was pretty sure that she was as an opaque film had covered the inside.

Technically, they were engaged, but what happened between him and Vasna seemed more like a "heat-of-the-moment" situation...situations...

He had a lot to think about, and thankfully the need to train her Kraul gave Tony some space from the woman to do just that. He emerged from the shower with a towel around his waist when someone rapped on his door. "Tony? It's important, I'm coming in," the voice on the other side declared.

Esava, one of the Celestial Elf Ascendants, a Rogue if he remembered correctly, barged into the room. "Please, do come in," Tony remarked.

Esava blushed but didn't look away. "The regeneration pod that the uh, woman that you brought back with you is in?" she asked more than stated.

Tony's heartbeat quickened. "What about it?"

"Well, it's uh, it's open now and she wants to see you," Esava said.

Tony paced the room. "How did she seem? Is she okay? Does she still have a hole in her chest? Is she mad at me?" The questions spilled out of his mouth before he could think them all through.

"Whoa, slow down, cowboy," Esava answered. She had crossed the room without Tony noticing and put her hands on his shoulders.

Definitely a Rogue, Tony thought.

"She seemed fine, a little confused, but she started asking for you right away. She just seems worried, Tony." Esava's silver eyes bored into his before they flicked down over his exposed skin. "You should probably just go see her and sort out whatever she might be 'mad' about in person."

"You're right," Tony said with a nod. "Thanks for letting me know." He went to leave and Esava grabbed him by the forearm.

"You should probably put on some clothes first," she said.

Tony looked down at himself and then back to Esava. "You know, you're right," he said. "So, maybe a little privacy, unless you planned on staying to watch," he added after a beat.

> Flirting: Critical Success!

Oh, come on! That was a joke!

The Celestial Elf turned a bright purple. "Auren was quite clear that you needed to be protected, the whole highest-level Ascendant thing," she replied.

Tony maintained the fake smile he plastered on his face and mentally kicked himself. *Alright, system, joking does **not** equal flirting, if I get that, you should!*

Fortunately, the Dog of War in the room was tall enough and curious enough about strangers to block Esava's prying eyes as Tony dressed. "Shall we?"

The trio moved through the corridors of the flagship with little interruption. Day by day the ship came back to life, the evidence of Tolik's betrayal and attack vanishing as the other Ascendants restored and made use of the space.

When they arrived at the primary regeneration room, Maximus and Esava hung back allowing Tony to go in ahead of them. The area around Jorogu's pod looked like a xenomorph hive from *Alien*. A slick grey film riddled with pock marks clung to the walls and where the pod *had* been was a cavernous overhang.

A pair of blazing green eyes snapped open in his direction from the darkness. "Jorogu?" Tony called.

"Tony?" she answered. The *clink* of her arachnid appendages moving across the metal flooring followed as Jorogu emerged. The tattered floral yukata was replaced by an armored bodysuit of burgundy chitin. Her spider legs, limbs capable of forming into deadly blades, looked to be more weapon-like than they had been. The final quarter of each leg had a spiral of serrations jutting out from it, there were matching blades on the outer edges of the bodysuit on Jorogu's wrists and ankles.

The Queen evolution had not only healed all her wounds, but clearly enhanced her offensive and defensive capabilities.

"You look... incredible," Tony remarked. "How do you feel?"

"A little foggy in here," she said, pointing to her head. "I'm having a hard time remembering what happened, how I got here... I was hoping you could fill in some of the blanks for me." She paused for a moment, Tony's remark registering fully in her addled brain. "And thank you." She blushed.

"What do you want to know? How can I help?"

"Well, I don't really remember anything that happened after." She paused, resting her left hand on her chest where the spike had run her through. "All that I know is from after I woke up in that pod, our borders have been pushed back by our enemies in the time that I was... recovering, there is infighting among the clusters, and my mother has passed her mantle on to me."

Tony's gut reaction was to ask, *"And who are those enemies?"* but he held the question back.

"Well, after you went down, I got up. It turns out that one of my enemies saw the duel with Sujuko as an opportunity to take me out, so he bestowed 'blessings' on him. When I saw that you weren't breathing I kind of lost it. Your mother held Sujuko and brought me back. We fought and I killed him."

Jorogu moved closer to Tony, retracting her spider legs to be on two feet. "So, how did we get here?"

"Semiramis told me that I had to save you and that she knew how. I... I followed her instructions which were to bring you back here and put you in the pod. The blade you gave me broke during the fight with Sujuko and after I finished the ritual it turned into this." Tony held up his right arm and his eyebrows shot to his hairline as he did. Covenant's color had changed to match Jorogu's chitin and a series of sharp blades protruded from the outside edge.

"The ritual? What ritual?" she asked, running her hands over the bracer and Tony's arm.

Tony hesitated, unsure if it would be better to go with the whole truth or to give more information over time. "I... I had to cut out your mother's heart and put it into your wound. That was the only way to save you and make sure that your people would go on."

Tears welled at the corners of Jorogu's eyes as they blazed with green flame. "That explains a lot." Her voice was barely above a whisper.

"Like what?"

"How I can hear the cries of my people, how I know exactly what hour it is on Arach, and how I know that Serketzi and her cyclone are the ones pressing the border."

"Serketzi? Who is that?"

"She is the recently crowned Queen of the Pandinus Swarm, we have… history." Jorogu took Tony's right arm in both of her hands, embossed above her left wrist was a matching sigil to the one she left on his right arm. Tony stared at it for a moment and flinched when a screen appeared in his vision.

Covenant		
Rarity: Unique (2 of 2) Durability: N/A Armor Slot: Wrist		
Type: Organic Attack Rating Bonus: +5 Defense Rating: +5		
The symbol of a continued Promise		
Special Effect: Connects the bearers of Covenant empathetically after a sacred bonding of flesh. Allows for reciprocal flow of: Emotional State, General Direction, Surface Thoughts		

Tony couldn't help but wonder if "a sacred bonding of flesh" would be recognized retroactively by the system. Jorogu wrapped Tony's arm around her like a shawl and leaned against him, resting her head against his chest.

"Thank you," she said.

"For what?" Tony asked.

Jorogu looked up at him with a playful scowl on her face, "For saving me, you brute!" She jabbed playfully into his gut and let her hand rest on his stomach.

"You've undergone quite the transformation while I was sleeping, haven't you?"

Jorogu traced the defined lines of Tony's abdominal muscles through his shirt. "What else happened?"

Tony gulped, he knew that this was going to come up eventually, but he had hoped to have the time to really *know* what he wanted to do about his unexplored engagement with Jorogu and the bond that he'd formed with Vasna.

He decided to stick to the basics for now, and explain more later, when his head was on straight. "When I came back from Arach it was discovered that a dungeon had formed on the flagship and was threatening control of the area, myself, Maximus, and another were tasked with finding and clearing the dungeon. Between defeating Sujuko and clearing the dungeon, my Essence ignited and I, well I guess you could say I evolved as a result."

Jorogu's head swiveled back and forth across the room's floor. "Where is the little not-snack?" she asked, some of the levity returning to her voice.

Tony let out a sharp whistle and Maximus padded around the corner. Jorogu tensed at first, prepared to defend herself, but the oscillating wag of the dog's tail and the gleam in Maximus's eyes swiftly reminded her of the pint-sized pup she had met.

"He has also grown!" she exclaimed, bounding over to meet the large dog and shower him with affection.

Tony smiled, glad that the two of them got along.

After the brief reunion, Jorogu closed her still-smoldering eyes and focused. An eloquent, flowing kimono materialized from viridian flames that wrapped around her, not as snug as the kimono she had worn before their duel, but still complementary to her curves with plenty of room for function. She approached Tony, her eyes locked with his and her body language was open.

"Don't worry, I haven't forgotten about you," she cooed. Jorogu closed the gap between them and pushed herself up into Tony's arms using her spider legs and planted her lips, and the whole front of her body, against his.

Covenant spread a warm flame throughout his whole body; the feeling was like sitting down in front of a fireplace after a two-mile walk in the snow and downing a cup of hot cider.

Still half-suspended in air, Jorogu pulled her mouth away from Tony's just enough to rest her forehead on his and licked her lips, savoring the embrace.

"Tell me, beloved, who is it that I taste on your lips?"

Epilogue

"What?!" Ignacious roared, a torrent of golden essence exploded from his golden tower.

"Y-yes m' lord. Tolik hasn't reported back and Mendacius is not responding to our hails," Sablo, the God-King's attendant sputtered.

"And this boy, the one we have tried to kill, twice on Arach and that our inside agent should have been more than capable of defeating, is the one you perceive to be responsible."

"It is the only reasonable-"

"There is *nothing* reasonable about that assumption, Sablo. The boy was a whelp. Send Pahadron after him the next time he's off the flagship. I want him dead."

"Yes m' lord,"

"And Sablo?" Ignacious said, "if that boy is not dead the next time you update me on the status of our agents in the program, you will be the next one sent to gather 'data' in the Abyss. Do I make myself clear?"

The attendant blanched, "Perfectly m' lord."

Backers

Denis Proulx

Sanryu

Thomas Rhoads

Stephen aka Scubaghost

The Original Ginger

L. H. Chapdelaine

Maegen McMorrow

Seantama

Kelsey Prince

Hoku

Bradley Ouelette

Bradford Wise

Jeff & Nancy Cole

Lance "Pike The Viking" Washburn

The Boggs Family

Twisted Nyx

Eduardio

The Horne Family

Vilagon

Megan G.